Jonas looked at her suspiciously. 'You can't possibl— be a virgin!'

'What diff— — r or not I've had ot—

'All the diff—erence in the world to me,' he said harshly.

'Why? Most men would be only too pleased to be a woman's first lover,' she retorted.

'Not this man,' he replied fervently.

Mac couldn't believe Jonas was refusing to make love to her just because she was a virgin!

'Why is that, Jonas?' she challenged. 'Do you think that I'm making such a grand gesture because I already imagine myself in love with you? Or do you think I'm trying to trap you in some way?'

Her eyes widened as she saw from the cold stiffening of his expression, the icy glitter of his eyes, that that was *exactly* what he thought—and so obviously feared...

Carole Mortimer was born in England, the youngest of three children. She began writing in 1978, and has now written over one hundred and fifty books for Harlequin Mills & Boon. Carole has six sons: Matthew, Joshua, Timothy, Michael, David and Peter. She says, 'I'm happily married to Peter senior; we're best friends as well as lovers, which is probably the best recipe for a successful relationship. We live in a lovely part of England.'

HIS CHRISTMAS VIRGIN

BY
CAROLE MORTIMER

MILLS & BOON

First published in Great Britain 2010
Harlequin Mills & Boon Limited,
Eton House, 18-24 Paradise Road, Richmond, Surrey TW9 1SR

© Carole Mortimer 2010

ISBN: 978 0 263 87854 7

Harlequin Mills & Boon policy is to use papers that are natural, renewable and recyclable products and made from wood grown in sustainable forests. The logging and manufacturing process conform to the legal environmental regulations of the country of origin.

Printed and bound in Spain
by Litografia Rosés, S.A., Barcelona

HIS CHRISTMAS VIRGIN

CHAPTER ONE

MAC came to an abrupt and wary halt halfway down the metal steps leading from the second floor of her warehouse-conversion home. She'd suddenly become aware of a large figure standing in the dark and shadowed alleyway beneath her.

A very large figure indeed, she noted with a frown as a man stepped out from those shadows to stand in the soft glow of light given out by the lamp shining behind her at the top of the staircase.

The man looked enormous from where Mac stood, his wide shoulders beneath the dark woollen overcoat that reached almost to his ankles adding to that impression. He had overlong dark hair brushed back from a hard and powerful face that at any other time Mac would have ached to put on canvas, light and piercing eyes— were they grey or blue?—and high cheekbones beside a long slash of a nose. He also possessed a perfectly sculptured mouth, the fuller bottom lip hinting at a depth of sensuality, and a firm and determined chin.

None of which was of the least importance—except maybe to the police, Mac wryly acknowledged to herself, if the man's reasons for being here turned out to be less than honest!

She repressed a shiver as the chill of the cold wind

of an early December evening began to seep into her bones. 'Can I help you?' she prompted sharply as she finished pulling on her cardigan, using both her hands to free the long length of her midnight-black hair from the collar. All the time wondering if she was going to have to use the ju-jitsu skills she had learnt during her years at university!

The man shrugged broad shoulders. 'Perhaps. If you can tell me whether or not Mary McGuire is at home?'

He knew her name!

Not that any of her friends ever called her Mary. But then, as Mac had never set eyes on this man before, he was hardly a friend, was he?

She glanced at the brightly lit studio behind and above her before turning to eye the man again guardedly. 'Who wants to know?'

'Look, I understand your wariness——'

'Do you?' she challenged.

'Of course,' he confirmed. 'I've obviously startled you, and I'm sorry for that, but I assure you my reasons for being here are perfectly legitimate. I simply wish to speak to Miss McGuire.'

'But does Miss McGuire wish to speak to you?'

The man gave a hard, humourless smile. 'I would hope so. Look, we could go back and forth like this all night.'

'I don't think so.' Mac shook her head, deciding that perhaps she wouldn't need to use those self-defence lessons on this man, after all. 'The Patels shut up shop in precisely ten minutes and I intend to be there before that.'

Dark brows rose over those light-coloured eyes. 'The Patels?'

Mac elaborated. 'They own the corner shop two streets away.'

'The significance of that being…?'

'I need to get some groceries before they close. That being the case, would you mind stepping aside so that I can get by?' She stepped down two more of the stairs so that they now stood at eye level.

Blue. His eyes were blue. A piercing electric blue.

Mac's breath caught in her throat as she stared into those mesmerising blue eyes, at the same time screamingly aware of the subtle and spicy smell of his aftershave or cologne. Of the leashed power he exuded. Even so, Mac was pretty sure she could take him; it was skill that mattered when it came to ju-jitsu, not size, and she was very skilled indeed.

The man looked at her beneath hooded lids. 'The fact that you're obviously leaving her home would seem to imply that you're a friend of Miss McGuire's.'

'Would it?'

Jonas deeply regretted the impulse of his decision to call and talk to Mary McGuire this evening. It would have been far more suitable, he now realised—and far less disturbing for one of the woman's friends—if he had simply telephoned first and made an appointment that was convenient to both of them. During the daylight hours, and hopefully at a time when one of her arty friends wasn't also visiting!

The fact that the thin little waif standing on the stairs had long, straight black hair that reached almost to her waist, and almond-shaped eyes of smoky-grey in a delicately beautiful face, took nothing away from the fact that she had obviously taken to heart the persona of the 'artist starving in a garret'!

As also evidenced by the overlarge dungarees she

wore over a white T-shirt, both articles of clothing covered by a baggy pink cardigan that looked as if it would wrap about the slenderness of her body twice. Her hands were tiny and thin, the skin almost translucent. The ratty blue canvas trainers on her feet were hardly suitable for the wet and icy early December weather, either.

Jonas had spent the last week in Australia on business. Successfully so, he acknowledged with inner satisfaction. Except he now felt the effects of this cold and damp English December right down to his bones, after the heat in Australia, despite wearing a thick cashmere overcoat over his suit.

This delicate-looking little waif must be even colder with only that thin cardigan as an outer garment. 'I apologise once again if I alarmed you just now.' He grimaced as he moved aside and allowed her to step down onto the pavement beside him.

The top of her head reached just under Jonas's chin as she looked up at him with obvious mockery. 'You didn't,' she came back glibly before wrapping her cardigan more tightly about her and hurrying off into the night.

Jonas was still watching her through narrowed lids as she stopped beneath the lamp at the corner of the street to glance back at him, her face a pale oval, that almost-waist-length hair gleaming briefly blue-black before she turned and disappeared around the corner.

He gave a rueful shake of his head before turning to ascend the metal steps that led up to Mary McGuire's studio; hopefully she wasn't going to be as unhelpful as her waiflike friend. Although he wouldn't count on it!

Mac lingered to chat with the Patels for a few minutes after she had bought her groceries. She liked the young couple who had opened this convenient mini-market two years ago, and Inda was expecting their first baby in a couple of months' time.

Mac's steps slowed as she saw the man who had spoken to her earlier sitting on the bottom step of the metal staircase waiting for her when she returned carrying her bag of groceries, those electric-blue eyes narrowing on her coldly as she walked towards him. 'I take it Miss McGuire wasn't in?' she asked lightly as she stopped in front of him.

It had been fifteen minutes since Jonas had reached the top of the metal staircase to ring the doorbell and receive no response. To knock on the door and get the same result. The blaze of lights in the studio told him that someone had to be home.

Or had very recently been so?

Leaving Jonas to pose the question as to whether or not the young woman in the dungarees and baggy pink cardigan, who had hurried off to the Patels' store to get groceries before they closed, was in fact Mary McGuire, rather than the visiting friend he had assumed her to be.

Something he found almost too incredible to believe!

This young woman looked half starved, and her clothes were more suited to someone living on the streets rather than the successful artist she now was; Mary McGuire had become an artist of some repute the last three years, her paintings becoming extremely valuable as serious collectors and experts alike waxed lyrical about the uniqueness of her style and use of colour.

Her reputation as an artist aside, the woman had also become the proverbial thorn in Jonas's side the last six months.

This woman?

He stood up slowly to look down at her critically as he took an educated guess on that being the case. 'Wouldn't it have just been easier to tell me that *you're* Mary McGuire?'

She gave a dismissive shrug of those thin and narrow shoulders. 'But not half as much fun.'

The hardening of Jonas's mouth revealed that he didn't appreciate being anyone's reason for having 'fun'. 'Now that we've established who you are, perhaps we could go upstairs and have a serious conversation?' he rasped coldly.

Smoky-grey eyes returned his gaze unblinkingly. 'No.'

He raised dark brows. 'What do you mean, *no*?'

'I mean no,' she repeated patiently. 'You may now know who I am but I still have no idea who you are.'

Jonas scowled darkly. 'I'm the man you've been jerking around for the past six months!'

Mac frowned up at him searchingly, only to become more positive than ever that she had never met this man before. At well over six feet tall, with those dark and dangerous good looks, he simply wasn't the sort of man that any woman, of any age, was ever likely to forget.

'Sorry.' She gave a firm shake of her head. 'I have absolutely no idea what you're talking about.'

That sculptured, sensual mouth twisted in derision. 'Does Buchanan Construction ring any bells with you?'

Alarm bells, maybe, Mac conceded as her gaze sharpened warily on the hard and powerful face above hers. A ruthless face, she now recognised warily. 'I take it Mr Buchanan has decided to send in one of his henchmen now that all attempts at polite persuasion have failed?'

Those blue eyes widened incredulously. 'You think I'm some sort of heavy sent to intimidate you?'

'Well, aren't you?' Mac bit out scathingly. 'So far I've had visits from Mr Buchanan's lawyer, his personal assistant, and his builder, so why not one of his henchmen?'

'Possibly because I don't employ any henchmen!' Jonas bit out icily, a nerve pulsing in his tightly clenched jaw as he glared down at her.

He had decided to come here personally this evening in the hope that he would be able to talk some sense into the reputed and respected—and mulishly stubborn—artist Mary McGuire, and instead he found himself being insulted by a five-foot-nothing scrap of a woman who had the dress sense of a bag-lady!

Those deep grey eyes had opened wide. '*You're* Jonas Buchanan?'

At last he had succeeded in shaking that mocking self-confidence a little. 'Surprised?' he taunted softly.

Surprised was definitely understating how Mac felt at that moment; stunned better described it.

She had known of Buchanan Construction—impossible not to, when for years there had been boards up on building sites all over London with that name emblazoned across them—when she was approached by the company's legal representative with an offer to buy her warehouse-conversion home.

Yes, Mac had certainly known the name Jonas Buchanan, and, if she had thought about it at all, she had always assumed that the owner of the worldwide construction company would be a man in his fifties or sixties, who probably enjoyed the occasional cigar with his brandy after no doubt indulging in a seven-course dinner.

The man now claiming to be Jonas Buchanan could only be in his mid-thirties at most, the healthy glow of his tanned face indicating that he didn't smoke even the occasional cigar, and the muscled and hard fitness of his body told her that he didn't indulge in seven-course dinners, either.

Mac looked up at him shrewdly. 'Do you have a driver's licence or something to prove that claim?'

Jonas scowled as his irritation deepened. He had travelled all over the world on business for years now, and never once during that time had anyone ever questioned that he was who he said he was. Until Mary McGuire, that was! 'Will a credit card do?' he snapped as he reached into the breast pocket of his overcoat for his wallet.

'I'm afraid not.'

Jonas's hand stilled. 'Why not?'

She shrugged in that ridiculously baggy pink cardigan. 'I need something with a photograph. Anyone could have a credit card with the name Jonas Buchanan printed on it.'

'You think I forged a credit card with Jonas Buchanan's name on it?' Jonas was incredulous.

'Or stole it.' She nodded. 'I would much rather see a passport or a driver's licence with a photograph on,' she stubbornly stuck to her guns.

Jonas's mouth compressed. 'On the basis, one supposes, that I haven't had either one of those forged in the name of Jonas Buchanan, too?'

She frowned. 'Hmm, I hadn't thought of that...'

No, he definitely shouldn't have given into impulse and come here this evening, Jonas acknowledged with ever-growing frustration as he pulled out the passport that he hadn't yet had the chance to remove from his pocket following his flight back from Sydney yesterday. He had stupidly allowed his success in Australia to convince him, after months of getting nowhere with the woman, that talking personally to Miss McGuire was the right way to handle this delicate situation!

'Here.' He thrust the passport at her.

Mac carefully avoided her fingers coming into contact with his as she took the passport and turned to the laminated photo page. Unlike her own passport photo, where she looked about sixteen and as if she ought to have a prisoner number printed beneath, this man's photograph showed him as exactly the lethally attractive and powerful man that he appeared in the flesh.

She quickly checked the details beside that photograph. Jonas Edward Buchanan. British citizen. His date of birth telling Mac that he had recently turned thirty-five.

She thought quickly as she slowly closed the passport before handing it back to him, knowing she could continue this game, and so annoy the hell out of this man, or… 'What can I do for you, Mr Buchanan?' she asked politely.

'Better,' he rasped impatiently as he stashed the passport back in his breast pocket. 'Obviously you and I need to talk, Miss McGuire—'

'I don't see why.' Mac brushed past him and began to ascend the stairs back up to her home, seeing no reason for her to linger out here in the cold now that she knew—or, at least, assumed—that this man wasn't about to mug her, after all. 'I'll be turning the light out at the top of the stairs in a minute or so; before I do, you might want to get back to the main streets where it's more brightly lit,' she advised without turning as she took the key from the pocket of her dungarees to unlock the door.

Jonas continued to look up at her in seething annoyance for a mere fraction of a second before following her, taking the stairs two at a time until he stood directly behind her. 'You and I need to talk,' he bit out between gritted teeth.

'Write me a letter,' she advised as she unlocked the door before stepping inside and turning to face him, her expression one of open challenge.

Jonas placed his hands on either side of the doorframe. 'I've already written you half a dozen letters. Letters you haven't bothered to reply to.'

She grimaced. 'There's always the possibility that I'll reply to the seventh.'

'I doubt that somehow,' Jonas accepted grimly. 'I don't think so!' He put his booted foot between the door and the frame as she would have closed that door in his face.

She opened it again to glare at him, those smoky grey eyes glittering darkly, bright colour in her normally pale cheeks. 'Remove your foot, Mr Buchanan, or you'll leave me with no choice but to call the police and have you forcibly removed from the premises!'

It was all too easy for Jonas to see that she was more angry than alarmed by his persistence. 'I only want the two of us to sit down and have a sensible conversation—'

'I'm busy.'

'I'm asking for two minutes of your time, damn it!' Jonas exclaimed.

Mac really wasn't being difficult when she said she was busy; she had a major exhibition at a gallery on

Saturday, only two days away, and she had one more painting to finish before then. Besides, no amount of talking to Jonas Buchanan was going to make her change her mind about selling the warehouse she had so lovingly worked on to make into her home.

Her grandfather had left this property to Mac when he died five years ago. It had been one of many warehouses by the river that had fallen into disuse as the trade into the London dock had fallen foul of other, more convenient transportation. Three floors high, it had been the perfect place for Mac to make into her home as well as her working studio. From the outside it still looked like an old warehouse, but inside the ground floor consisted of a garage and utility room, the second floor was her living quarters, and the third floor made a spacious studio.

Unfortunately, the area where the warehouse stood had recently become very attractive to property developers such as Jonas Buchanan, as they bought up the run-down riverside properties to put up blocks of luxurious apartments that had the added allure of a magnificent and uninterrupted view of the river.

It was this man's bad luck that Mac's own warehouse home stood on one of those sites.

She sighed. 'I've already given my answer to your lawyer, your personal assistant, and your builder,' she reminded him pointedly. 'I don't want to sell. Not now. Not in the future. Not ever. Is that clear enough for you?'

Jonas Buchanan's expression was one of pure exasperation as he gave an impatient shake of his head. 'You must realise that the area around you is going to become a noisy building site over the winter months?'

She shrugged. 'You've fenced off this area for that purpose.'

He frowned. 'That isn't going to lessen the noise of lorries arriving with supplies. Workmen constantly hammering and banging as the buildings start to go up, followed by huge cranes being erected on site. Exactly how do you expect to still be able to work with all that going on?'

Mac's eyes narrowed. 'The same way I've continued to work the last few months as you've systematically pulled down all the buildings around this one.'

Jonas's mouth firmed at the implied criticism. 'I offered several times to relocate you—'

'I have no wish to be "relocated", Mr Buchanan,' Mary McGuire growled out between clenched teeth. 'This is my *home*. It will remain my home still, even once you've built and sold your luxurious apartments.'

And, as Jonas was only too aware, be a complete eyesore to the people who lived in those exclusive multimillion-pound apartments! 'In my experience, everyone has a price, Mary—'

'Mac.'

He frowned. 'Sorry?'

'Everyone who actually knows me calls me Mac, not Mary,' she explained. 'And maybe the people you're acquainted with have "a price", Mr Buchanan,' she said scathingly, smoky-grey eyes glittering with contempt. 'I happen to believe that my own family and friends have more integrity than that. As do I!'

Jonas now fully understood the frustration his employees had previously encountered when trying to talk to Mary 'Mac' McGuire; he had never before met a more stubborn, pigheaded and unreasonable individual than this particular woman!

His mouth thinned. 'You know where to reach me when you change your mind.'

'*If* I change my mind,' she corrected firmly. 'Which I won't. Now, if you will excuse me, Mr Buchanan?' She raised ebony brows. 'I really am very busy.'

And Jonas wasn't? With millions of pounds invested in one building project or another all over the world, Jonas's own time was, and always had been, at a premium. He certainly didn't have any more of it to waste tonight on this woman.

He stepped back. 'As I said, you know where to reach me when you've had enough.'

'Goodnight, Mr Buchanan,' she shot back with saccharin—and pointed—sweetness, before quietly closing the door in his face.

Jonas continued to scowl at that closed door for several minutes after she had carried out her threat to turn off the outside light and left him in darkness apart from the lights visible inside the warehouse itself.

He had already invested too much time and money in the building project due to begin on this site in the New Year to allow one stubborn individual to ruin it for him, or Buchanan Construction.

Obviously the money he had so far offered for this property wasn't enough of a reason for Miss McGuire to agree to move. Which meant Jonas was going to have to come up with a more convincing reason for her to want to leave.

CHAPTER TWO

'CHEER up, Mac,' Jeremy Lyndhurst teased as the first of the guests invited to this evening's viewing began to come through the gallery. The fifty-something co-owner of the prestigious Lyndwood Gallery continued, 'A few hours of looking good and being socially polite this evening, and tomorrow you can go back to being reclusive and dressing like a tramp!'

Mac chuckled huskily—as she knew she was meant to—at this reminder of the affront it was to Jeremy's own impeccable dress sense whenever she turned up at his gallery in her paint-smeared working clothes. Which she had done a lot the last few weeks as she came to deliver the individual paintings due to be exhibited at this evening's 'invitation only' showing of her work.

Jeremy's partner—in more ways than one—Magnus Laywood, a tall, blond giant in his forties, was at the door to 'meet and greet' as more of those guests began to arrive; mainly art critics and serious collectors, but also some other individuals who were just seriously rich.

There were twenty of Mac's paintings on show this evening, and all of them expertly displayed by Jeremy and Magnus, on walls of muted cream with their own individual lighting so that they showed to their best advantage.

It was the first individual exhibition of its kind that Mac had ever agreed to do—and now that the evening had finally arrived she was so nervous her knees were knocking together!

'Here, drink this.' Jeremy picked up a glass of champagne from one of the waiters who were starting to circulate amongst the guests in the rapidly filling room, and handed it to her. 'Your face just went green!' he explained with a chuckle.

Mac took a restorative sip of the bubbly alcohol. 'I've never been so nervous in my entire life.'

'Oh, to be twenty-seven again,' Jeremy murmured mournfully.

Mac took another sip of the delicious champagne. 'What if they don't like my work?' she wailed.

'They can't all be idiots, darling,' Jeremy drawled. 'It's going to be a wonderful evening, Mac,' he reassured her seriously as she still looked unconvinced. 'I know how hard this is for you, love, but just try to enjoy it, hmm?'

The problem was that Mac had never been particularly fond of exhibiting her work. Selling it, yes. Showing it to other people, and being 'socially polite' to those people, no. Unfortunately, as Mac was well aware, she couldn't make a living from her paintings if she didn't sell them.

'I'll try— Oh. My. God!' she gasped weakly as she saw, and easily recognised, the man now standing beside the door engaged in conversation with Magnus.

Jonas Buchanan!

He was as tall as Magnus, and dark and dangerous where the other man was blond and amiable, there was no mistaking that overlong dark hair and those hard and chiselled features dominated by piercing blue eyes that now swept coldly over the other guests.

Mac's heart hammered loudly in her chest as she took in the rest of his appearance. Dressed like every other man in the room, in a tailored black evening suit and snowy white shirt with a perfectly arranged black bow-tie at his throat, Jonas nevertheless somehow managed to look so much more compellingly handsome than any other man in the room.

'What is it?' Jeremy followed her line of vision. 'Who is that?' he murmured appreciatively, his longstanding relationship with Magnus not rendering him immune to the attractions of other men.

Mac dragged her gaze away from Jonas to look accusingly at the co-owner of the Lyndwood Gallery. 'You should know—you invited him!'

'I don't think so.' Jeremy's eyes were narrowed as he continued to look across at Jonas. 'Who is he?'

Mac swallowed hard before answering. 'Jonas Buchanan.'

Jeremy looked impressed. '*The* Jonas Buchanan?'

As far as Mac was aware there was only one Jonas Buchanan, yes!

'Ah, I understand now.' Jeremy nodded his satisfaction as a puzzle was obviously solved. 'He's with Amy Walters.'

Mac turned back in time to see Jonas Buchanan placing a proprietary hand beneath the elbow of a tall and beautiful redhead, the two of them talking softly together as they crossed the room to join a group of guests, Jonas easily standing several inches taller than the other men. Mac turned away abruptly.

'Amy's the art critic for *The Individual*,' Jeremy

supplied dryly as he saw the blankness of Mac's expression.

A completely unnecessary explanation as far as Mac was concerned; she knew exactly who Amy Walters was. It was the fact that the other woman had brought Jonas with her this evening, a man Mac was predisposed to dislike, that made things more than a little awkward; Mac was only too aware that she would have to be polite to the beautiful art critic if the two of them were introduced. Something that might be a little difficult for her to do with the arrogantly self-assured Jonas Buchanan standing at Amy's side!

The reason for that current self-assurance was obvious; invitations to this exhibition had been sent out weeks ago to ensure maximum attendance. Meaning that Jonas Buchanan had to have known, when they had met and spoken so briefly together two evenings ago, that he was going to be at her exhibition at the Lyndwood Gallery this evening.

Rat!

If he thought he could intimidate her by practically gatecrashing her exhibition, then he could—

'How nice to see you again so soon, Mac.'

Mac stiffened, her earlier nervousness completely evaporating and being replaced by indignation as she recognised Jonas Buchanan's silkily sarcastic tone as he spoke softly behind her.

Double rat!

Jonas kept his expression deliberately neutral as Mary 'Mac' McGuire slowly turned to face him.

To say that he had been surprised by her appearance this evening would be a complete understatement! In fact, if Amy hadn't teasingly assured him that the delicately lovely woman with her ebony hair secured on top of her head to reveal the slender loveliness of her neck, and wearing a red Chinese-style knee-length silk dress with matching red high-heeled sandals that showed off her shapely legs to perfection, was indeed the artist herself, then Jonas wasn't sure he would have even recognised her!

She looked totally different with her hair up, older, more sophisticated, those mysterious smoky-grey eyes surrounded by long and thick dark lashes, the paleness of her cheeks highlighted with blusher, those full and sensuous lips outlined with a lip gloss the same vibrant red as that figure-hugging red silk gown and three-inch sandals.

In a word, she looked exquisite!

Whoever would have thought it? Jonas mused ruefully. From bag-lady to femme fatale with the donning of a red silk dress.

Although the challenging glitter in those smoky grey eyes as she glared up at him was certainly familiar enough. 'Mr Buchanan,' she greeted dryly. 'Jeremy, this is Jonas Buchanan. Jonas, one of the gallery owners, Jeremy Lyndhurst.'

Mac watched through narrowed lashes as the two men shook hands, finding Jonas's appearance even more disturbing tonight than she had two evenings ago. He was one of the few men she had met who wore the elegance of a black evening suit rather than the clothes wearing him, the power of his personality such that it was definitely the man one noticed rather than the superb tailoring of the clothing he wore.

'Have you managed to lose Miss Walters already?' Mac asked sweetly as she saw that the other woman was talking animatedly to another man across the room.

Those electric-blue eyes darkened with sudden humour. 'Amy pretty much does her own thing,' Jonas Buchanan replied with a singular lack of concern.

'How…understanding, of you,' Mac taunted. Really, she was nervous enough about this evening already, without having to suffer this particular man's presence!

'Not at all,' Jonas drawled with deepening amusement.

'I do hope you will both excuse me…?' Jeremy cut in apologetically. 'Someone has just arrived that I absolutely have to go and talk to.'

'Of course,' Jonas Buchanan accepted smoothly. 'I assure you, I'm only too happy to stay and keep Mac company,' he added as he took a deliberate step closer to her.

A close proximity that Mac instantly took exception to!

One or other of this man's associates had been hounding her for months now in an effort to buy her home—but only so that it could be knocked down to become part of the area of ground landscaped as a garden for the new luxury apartment complex. The fact that Jonas Buchanan himself had now decided to get in on the act did not impress Mac in the slightest.

'You're looking very beautiful this evening—'

'Don't let appearances deceive you, Mr Buchanan,' she interrupted sharply. 'I'll be back to wearing my dungarees tomorrow.' Mac had made the mistake of dating a prestigious and arrogant art critic when she was still at university, and she wasn't about to ever let another man treat her as nothing but a beautiful trophy to exhibit on his arm. 'Exactly what are you doing here, Mr Buchanan?' she asked him directly.

Jonas studied her through narrowed lids. Two evenings ago he had thought this woman looked like a starving waif with absolutely no dress sense, but her exquisite appearance tonight in the red silk dress—which Jonas realised almost every other man in the room was also aware of—indicated to him that she must actually dress in those other baggy and unflattering clothes because she wanted to.

He shrugged. 'Amy asked me to be her escort this evening.'

Those red-glossed lips curled with distaste. 'How flattering to have a woman ask you out.'

Jonas's gaze hardened. 'I'm always happy to spend the evening with my cousin.'

Those smoky-grey eyes widened. 'Amy Walters is your cousin?'

He arched a mocking brow at her obvious incredulity. 'Is that so hard to believe?'

Well, no, of course it wasn't hard to believe, Mac accepted uncomfortably. But it did mean that Jonas wasn't here this evening on a date with another woman, as Mac had assumed that he was...

And why should that matter to her? She had no personal interest in this man. Did she...?

Lord, she hoped not!

The fact that he was one of the most compellingly attractive men Mac had ever met was surely nullified by the fact that he was also the man trying to force her out of her own home, by the sheer act of making it too uncomfortable for her to stay?

She steadily returned Jonas's piercing gaze as she shrugged. 'I don't see any family resemblance.'

He smiled wickedly. 'Maybe that's because Amy is a woman and I'm a man?'

Mac was well aware that Jonas was a man. Much too aware for her own comfort, as it happened. At five feet two inches tall, and weighing only a hundred pounds, in stark contrast to Jonas Buchanan's considerable height and powerful build, she was made totally aware of her own femininity by this man. And, uncomfortably, her vulnerability...

Her mouth firmed. 'I really should go and circulate amongst the other guests,' she told him as she placed her empty champagne glass down on a side table with the intention of leaving.

'Maybe I'll come with you.' Jonas Buchanan reached out to lightly grasp Mac by the elbow as she would have turned away.

His touch instantly sent a quiver of shocking awareness along the length of her arm and down into her breasts, causing them to swell inside her bra and the nipples to engorge to a pleasurable ache against the lacy material.

It was a completely unfamiliar—and unwelcome—feeling to Mac. After that one brief disaster of a relationship while at university, she had spent the following six years concentrating solely on her painting career, with little or no time to even think about relationships. She wasn't thinking of one now, either. Jonas Buchanan was the last man—positively *the* last man!—that Mac should be feeling physically attracted to.

Her body wasn't listening to her, unfortunately, as the warmth of Jonas's hand on her arm began to infiltrate the rest of her body, culminating uncomfortably at the apex of her thighs as she felt herself moisten there, in such a burst of heat that she gasped softly in awareness of that arousal.

She raised startled eyes to that hard and compellingly handsome face above hers, Jonas standing so close to her now she was able to see the individual pores in his skin. To recognise the lighter blue ring that surrounded the iris of his eyes, which gave them that piercing appearance. To gaze hypnotically at those slightly parted lips as they slowly lowered towards hers—

Mac jerked herself quickly out of his grasp. 'What are you doing?'

Yes, what *was* he doing? Jonas wondered frowningly. For a brief moment he had forgotten that they were surrounded by noisily chatting art critics and collectors. Had felt as if he and the exquisitely beautiful Mac McGuire were the only two people in the room, surrounded only by an expectant awareness and the heady seduction of her perfume.

Damn it, Jonas had been so unaware of those other people in the room that he had been about to kiss her in front of them all!

Her appearance this evening was an illusion, he reminded himself. Tonight she was the artist, deliberately dressed to beguile and seduce art critics and art collectors alike into approving of or buying her paintings. The fact that she had almost succeeded in seducing him into forgetting exactly who and what she was only increased Jonas's feelings of self-disgust.

His mouth thinned as he stepped away to look down at her through hooded lids. 'I really shouldn't keep you from your other guests any longer.'

Mac trembled slightly at the contempt she could hear in Jonas's tone. As she wondered what she had done to incur that contempt; he had been the one about to kiss her and not the other way around!

Her gaze returned to those sensually sculptured lips as she wondered what it would have felt like to have them part and claim her own lips. Jonas's mouth looked hard and uncompromising now, but seconds ago those

firm lips had been soft and inviting as they lowered
to hers—

Get a grip, Mac, she instructed herself firmly as she
straightened decisively. The fact that he looked wonderful in a black evening suit, and was one of the most
gorgeous men she had ever set eyes on, did not detract
from the fact that he was also the enemy!

She eyed him mockingly. 'I would be polite and
say that it's been nice seeing you again, Mr Buchanan,
but we both know I would be lying…' She trailed off
pointedly.

He gave a humourless smile in recognition of that
mockery.

'I doubt very much that you've seen the last of me,
Mac.'

She raised dark brows. 'I sincerely hope that you're
wrong about that.'

His smile deepened. 'I rarely am when it comes to
matters of business.'

'Modest too,' Mac scorned. 'Is there no end to your
list of talents?' She snorted delicately. 'If you'll excuse
me, Mr Buchanan.' She didn't wait for his reply to her
statement but moved to cross the room to where she
realised Magnus had discreetly been trying to attract
her attention for the past few minutes.

Jonas stood unmoving as he watched her progress
slowly across the room, stopping occasionally to greet
people she knew. Unlike her behaviour towards him, the
smiles Mac bestowed on the other guests were warm
and relaxed, the huskiness of her laugh a soft caress to
the senses, and revealing small, even white teeth against
those full and red-glossed lips.

The tight-fitting silk dress emphasised the rounded
curve of her bottom as she moved, and the slit up the

side of the gown revealed the shapely length of her thigh. Jonas scowled his disapproval as he saw that most of the men in the room were also watching her, with one persistent man even grasping her wrist and trying to engage her in conversation before she laughingly managed to extricate herself and walked away to join Magnus Laywood.

'So what did you make of our little artist…?'

Jonas turned to look at Amy, compressing his mouth in irritation as he realised he had been so engrossed in watching Mac that he hadn't noticed his cousin's approach. A tall and beautiful redhead, with a temper to match, Jonas's maternal cousin wasn't a woman men usually overlooked!

'What did I think of Mary McGuire?' Jonas played for time as he was still too surprised at his reaction to the artist's change in appearance to be able to formulate a satisfactory answer to Amy's archly voiced question. 'She seems…a little young, to have engendered all this interest,' he drawled with bored lack of interest as he took two glasses of champagne from the tray of a passing waiter and handed one of them to his cousin.

'Young but brilliant,' Amy assured him unreservedly as she sipped the chilled wine.

'High praise indeed,' Jonas mused; his cousin wasn't known for her effusiveness when it came to her job as art critic for *The Individual*.

Amy linked her arm with his encouragingly. 'Come and look at some of her paintings.'

Mac continued to chat lightly with a collector who had expressed a serious interest in buying one of the paintings on display, at the same time completely aware of Jonas Buchanan and his cousin as they moved slowly through the two-roomed gallery to view her work.

It was impossible to tell from Jonas's expression what he thought of her paintings, those blue eyes hooded as he studied each canvas, his mouth unsmiling as he murmured in soft reply to Amy Walters's comments.

He probably hated them, Mac accepted heavily as she politely tried to refer the flirtatious collector to Jeremy for the more serious discussion over price. No doubt Jonas preferred modern art as opposed to her more ethereal style and bright but slightly muted use of colour. No doubt he had only agreed to accompany his cousin this evening in the first place because he had known that by doing so he would undermine Mac's confidence.

He needn't have bothered—Mac already hated all of this! She disliked the artificiality. Found the inane chatter tiresome. And she found herself especially irritated by the opportunistic collector she now realised was unobtrusively trying to place his hand on her bottom…

Mac moved sharply away from him, her eyes snapping with indignation at the uninvited familiarity. 'I'm sure that you'll find Jeremy will be only too happy to help with any further questions you might have.'

The middle-aged man chuckled meaningfully as he moved closer. 'He isn't my type!'

Mac frowned her discomfort, at a complete loss as to how to deal with this situation without causing a scene. Something she knew was out of the question with a dozen or so reporters also present in the room.

In their own individual ways Jeremy and Magnus had worked as hard on producing this exhibition this evening as Mac had. If she were to slap this obnoxious man's face, as she was so tempted to do, then the headlines in some of tomorrow's newspapers would read 'Artist slaps buyer's face!' instead of any praise or constructive criticism on her actual work.

She gave a shake of her head. 'I really don't think—'

'Sorry to have been gone so long, darling,' Jonas Buchanan interrupted smoothly as his arm moved firmly about Mac's waist to pull her securely against his side. He gave the other man a challenging smile, those compelling blue eyes as hard as the sapphires they resembled. 'It's rather crowded in here, isn't it?'

'I—yes.' The older and shorter man looked disconcerted by this unmistakable show of possessiveness. 'I—If you will both excuse me? I'll take your advice, Mac, and go and discuss the details with Jeremy.' He turned to hurriedly disappear into the crowd.

Mac found that she was trembling in reaction—and was totally at a loss to know if it was caused by the unpleasantness of the last minute or so, or because Jonas still held her so firmly against him that she was totally aware of the hard warmth of his powerful body…

Jonas took one look down at Mac's white face before his arm tightened about her waist and he turned her towards the entrance to the gallery. 'Let's get some air,' he suggested as he all but lifted her off the floor to carry her across the room and out of the door into the icy cold night. Something he instantly realised was a mistake as he could see by the street-lamp how Mac had begun to shiver in the thin silk dress. 'Here.' He slipped off his jacket to place it about her shoulders, his thumbs brushing lightly against the warm swell of her breasts as he stood in front of her to pull the lapels together.

Her eyes were huge as she looked up at him. 'Now you're going to be cold.'

She looked like a little girl playing dress-up with the shoulders of Jonas's jacket drooping down at the sides and the bulky garment reaching almost down to her knees. Except there was nothing childlike about the sudden awareness that darkened those smoky-grey eyes, or the temptation of those parted red-glossed lips as she breathed shallowly.

'How old are you really?' Jonas rasped harshly.

She blinked. 'I— What does that have to do with anything?'

He gave an impatient shrug of his shoulders. 'When I met you the other night you looked like someone's little sister. Tonight you look—well, tonight you look more like most men wished their best friend's little sister looked!'

She tilted that long elegant neck as she looked up at him. 'And how is that?' she prompted huskily.

This is a bad idea, Buchanan, Jonas cautioned himself. A very, very bad idea, he warned firmly even as his fascinated gaze remained fixed on those moist and parted lips.

A taste. He just wanted a taste of those sexy red lips—

Hell, no!

He was trying to transact a business deal with this woman, and he made a point of never mixing business with pleasure. And Jonas had no doubts it would have been very pleasurable to touch and taste those full and pouting lips with his own...

His expression was deliberately taunting as he looked down at her. 'In that dress you look like a woman who's ready for hot and wild sex.'

Mac's eyes widened as she gasped at the insult. 'I'll wear what I damn well please!'

That blue gaze moved deliberately down to the split in the side of her dress that revealed the long, bare length of her silky thigh. 'Obviously.'

'You're no better than the idiot whose attentions you

just appeared to save me from,' she accused furiously
as she pulled his jacket from about her shoulders and
almost threw it back at him before turning on her heel
and marching back into the gallery without so much as
a second glance.

Rude. Obnoxious. Insulting. Rat!

CHAPTER THREE

'I DON'T give a damn whether Mr Buchanan is busy or not,' an angry voice—that unfortunately Jonas recognised only too well!—snapped in the outer office of his London headquarters at nine-thirty on Monday morning. 'No, I have no intention of making an appointment. I want to talk to him *now*!' The door between the two rooms was flung open as Mac burst into Jonas's office.

Jonas barely had time to register her appearance, in a fitted black jumper and faded hipster blue denims, her hair a silken ebony curtain over her shoulders and down the length of her spine, before she marched over to stand in front of his desk, her cheeks flushed and eyes fever bright as she glared across at him.

She looked like a feral cat—and just as ready to spit and claw!

Jonas tilted his head sideways in order to look over at his secretary as she stood hesitantly in the doorway. 'There's no need to call Security, Mandy,' he drawled. 'I'm sure Miss McGuire won't be staying long…' He looked up enquiringly at Mac as he added that last statement.

Her eyes narrowed menacingly and she seemed to literally breathe fire at him. 'Long enough to tell you exactly what I think of you and your strong-arm tactics, at least!' she snarled.

'Thanks, Mandy,' Jonas dismissed his secretary, waiting until she had quietly left the room before looking back at Mac. 'You appear to be a little…distraught, this morning?'

'Distraught!' she echoed incredulously. 'I'm *furious*!'

Jonas could clearly see that. He just had no idea why that was.

Thankfully Amy had been ready to leave the gallery on Saturday evening when Jonas returned, allowing no opportunity for him and Mac to engage in any more arguments. Or to tempt Jonas into wanting to kiss her…

In the thirty-six hours since Jonas had last seen Mac, he had managed to convince himself that temptation had been an aberration on his part, a purely male reaction to the fact that she had looked as sexy as hell in that red silk dress.

Except that he now found himself facing the same temptation!

Mac wasn't wearing any make-up today, and her hair was windblown, her clothes casual in the extreme—and yet he still found his gaze drawn again and again to the fullness of her tempting lips.

Jonas's fingers tightened about the pen he was holding. 'Perhaps you would care to tell me why you're so furious?' he asked harshly. 'And what it has to do with me,' he added.

'Oh, don't worry, I'm going to tell you exactly why,' Mac promised. 'And you know damn well what it has to do with you!' she said accusingly.

Jonas raised his palms. 'I really am very busy this morning, Mac—'

'Do you have someone else you need to go and intimidate?' she scorned. 'Oh, I forgot—you usually leave that sort of thing to your underlings!' She snorted disgustedly. 'Well, let me assure you that I don't scare that easily—'

'Would you just calm down and tell me what the hell you're talking about?' he cut in coldly, those blue eyes glacial.

Mac was breathing hard, too upset still to heed the warning she could see in that chilling gaze. 'You know *exactly* what I'm talking about—'

'If I did, I would hardly be asking you to explain, now, would I?' Jonas retorted.

Mac's gaze narrowed. 'You knew I wouldn't be at home on Saturday evening because of the exhibition, and you shamelessly took advantage of that fact. You—'

He threw his pen down on the desktop before standing up impatiently. 'Mac, if you don't stop throwing out accusations, and just explain yourself, I'm afraid I'm going to have to ask you to leave.'

The anger Mac was feeling had been brewing, growing, since she'd returned home on Saturday evening. Having no idea where Jonas Buchanan actually lived, she'd had to spend all of Sunday brooding too, with only the promise of being able to visit Jonas at his office first thing on Monday morning to sustain her. Having his secretary try to stonewall her had done nothing to improve Mac's mood.

She drew in a controlling breath. 'My studio was broken into on Saturday evening. But, then, you already knew that, didn't you?' she said pointedly. 'You—'

'Stop right there!' Jonas thundered as he stepped out from behind his desk.

Mac instinctively took a step backwards as he

38   CAROLE MORTIMER

towered over her, appearing very dark and threatening in a charcoal-grey suit, pale grey shirt and grey silk tie, with that overlong dark hair styled back from the chiselled perfection of his face.

Those sculptured lips firmed to a livid thin line. 'You're telling me that your studio was broken into while you were out at the exhibition on Saturday evening?'

'You know that it was—'

'Mac, if you're going to continue to accuse me like this then I would seriously suggest that you have the evidence to back it up!' he warned harshly. 'Do you have that evidence?' he pressed.

She shook her head. 'The police didn't find anything that would directly implicate you, no,' she admitted grudgingly. 'But then, they wouldn't have done, would they?' she rallied. 'You're much more clever—'

'*Mac!*'

She blinked at the steely coldness Jonas managed to project into just that one word. Shivered slightly at the icy warning she could read in his expression.

But she didn't care how cold and steely Jonas was, the break-in had to have been carried out by someone who worked for him. Who else would have bothered, would have a reason to break into a building that, from the outside, appeared almost derelict?

Jonas was hanging onto his own temper by a thread. Angered as much by the thought of someone having broken into Mac's home at all, as at the accusations she was making about him being responsible for that break-in. She could so easily have been at home on Saturday evening. Could have been seriously hurt if she had disturbed the intruder.

He frowned. 'Did they take anything?'

'Not that I can see, no. But—'

'Let's just stick to the facts, shall we, Mac?' Jonas bit out, a nerve pulsing in his tightly clenched jaw.

She eyed him warily. 'The facts are that I arrived home late on Saturday evening to find my studio completely wrecked. The only consolation—if it can be called that!—is that at least all of my most recent work was at the gallery that evening.'

Jonas nodded. 'So there was no real damage done?'

Mac's eyes widened indignantly. 'My home, my privacy, was invaded!'

And he could understand how upsetting that must have been for her. Must still be. But the facts were that neither Mac nor her property had actually come to any real harm.

He moved to sit on the side of his desk. 'At least you had the sense to call the police.'

'I'm not a complete moron!'

Jonas didn't think that Mac was a moron at all. All evidence was to the contrary. 'I don't recall ever saying otherwise,' he commented dryly.

'You implied it, with your "at least" comment!' She thrust her hands into the hip pockets of her denims, instantly drawing Jonas's attention to the full and mature curve of her breasts beneath the fitted black sweater. Making a complete nonsense of how he had mistaken her for a young girl at their first meeting two days ago.

She was different again today, he realised ruefully. No longer the waif or the femme fatale, but a beautiful and attractive woman in her late twenties. A man could never become bored with Mac McGuire when he would never know on any given day which woman he was going to meet!

He sighed. 'What conclusions did the police come to?'

She shrugged those narrow shoulders. 'They seem to think it was kids having fun.'

Jonas grimaced. 'Maybe they're right—'

'Kids don't just break in, they steal things,' Mac disagreed impatiently. 'I have a forty-two-inch flat-screen television set, a new Blu-ray Disc player, a state-of-the-art music system and dozens of CDs, and none of them were even touched.'

Jonas looked intrigued. 'So it was just your studio that was targeted?'

'*Just* my studio?' she repeated indignantly. 'You just don't understand, do you?' she added as she turned away in disgust.

The problem for Jonas was that he did understand. He understood only too well. Having seen Mac's work for himself on Saturday evening, he knew exactly how important her studio was to her. It was the place where she created beauty deep from within her. Where she poured out her soul onto canvas. To have that vandalised, wrecked, was the equivalent of attacking the inner, deeply emotional Mac.

His mouth firmed. 'But you believe *I'm* responsible for what happened?'

Mac turned to eye him warily as she once again heard that underlying chill in Jonas's tone, the warning against repeating her earlier accusations.

If Jonas wasn't responsible, then who was? Not just who, but why? Nothing of value had been taken. In fact, the living-area part of her home hadn't been touched. Only her studio had been vandalised. Surely whoever had done that would have to know her to realise that the studio was her heart and soul?

Which, as he didn't know her, surely ruled out Jonas Buchanan as being the person responsible for the damage? After all, they had only met twice before this morning, and neither of those occasions had been in the least conducive to them gaining any personal insights about each other. Jonas certainly couldn't know how much Mac's studio meant to her.

She gave a weary shake of her head. 'I don't know what to believe any more…'

'That's something, I suppose,' Jonas commented dryly. 'Why don't we start with the premise that neither I nor anyone I employ had anything to do with the break-in, and go from there?' he suggested. 'Who else could have reason for wanting to cause you this personal distress? Perhaps an artist rival, jealous of your success? Or maybe an ex-lover who didn't go quietly?' he added.

Mac's eyes narrowed. 'Very funny!'

Strangely, Jonas didn't find his last suggestion in the least amusing. Especially when it was accompanied by vivid images of this woman's naked body intimately entwined with another man, that ebony hair falling about the two of them like a silken curtain…

He straightened abruptly and once again moved to sit behind his desk. 'I really am busy this morning, Mac. In fact I have an appointment in a little under five minutes, so why don't we meet up again at lunchtime and discuss this further?'

Mac eyed him suspiciously. 'You're inviting me out to lunch?' she repeated uncertainly, as if she were sure she must have misheard him.

No, Jonas hadn't been inviting her out to lunch. In fact, those earlier imaginings had already warned him that, the less he had to do with the volatile Mac McGuire, the better he would like it!

'On second thoughts it would be far more sensible if you were to talk to my secretary on your way out and make an appointment to come back and see me at a time more convenient for both of us.'

It would be more sensible, Mac agreed, but after arriving back late from the gallery on Saturday evening to find her studio in chaos, and then another hour spent talking to the police, to spend the rest of the weekend alternating between ranting at the mess and crying for the same reason, she wanted to sort this problem out once and for all. Today, if possible.

Her parents, safely ensconced in their retirement bungalow home in Devon, where they also ran a B&B in the summer months, already worried that their move to the south of England had left her living alone in London. They would be horrified to learn that she'd had a break-in at her home.

But was it a good idea for her to have lunch with Jonas Buchanan? Probably not, Mac acknowledged ruefully. Except that he had seemed sincere—no, furious, actually—in his denial that he was in any way responsible for the break-in.

If that were genuinely the case, then she probably owed him an apology, at least, for having come here and made those bitter accusations.

'Lunch sounds a better idea,' Mac contradicted his earlier suggestion. 'In fact, I'll take you out to lunch.'

Jonas raised mocking brows. 'Would that offer be the equivalent of wearing sackcloth and ashes?'

Mac felt the warmth of colour in her cheeks at his pointed suggestion that she should appear penitent for her behaviour. 'It means that for the moment I'm prepared to give you the benefit of the doubt regarding the break-in.'

'For the moment?' Jonas repeated softly, trying not to grit his teeth. 'That's very…good of you.'

'Don't push your luck, Jonas,' she snapped. 'I'm only suggesting this at all because this whole situation seems to be getting out of control.'

Jonas considered her between hooded lids. Mac really had behaved like a little hellion this morning by forcing her way into his office and throwing out her wild accusations. And if Jonas had any sense then he would tell her he would see her in court for even daring to voice those accusations without a shred of evidence to back up her claim. He certainly shouldn't even be thinking of accepting her invitation to have lunch.

Except that he was…

Mac intrigued him. Piqued his interest in a way no woman had done for a very long time. If ever.

All the more reason not to even consider going out to lunch with her then!

She was absolutely nothing like the women Jonas was usually attracted to. Beautiful and sophisticated women who knew exactly what the score was. Who expected nothing from him except the gift of a few expensive baubles during the few weeks or months their relationship lasted; if any of those women had ever harboured the hope of having any more than that from him then they had been sadly disappointed.

Jonas had witnessed and lived through the disintegration of his own parents' marriage. He had been twelve years old when he'd watched them start to rip each other to shreds, both emotionally and verbally, culminating in an even messier divorce when Jonas was fifteen.

He had decided long ago that none of that was for

him. Not the initial euphoria of falling in love. Followed by a few years of questionable happiness. Before the compromises began. The irritation. And then finally the hatred for each other, followed by divorce.

Jonas wanted none of it. Would willingly forgo the supposed 'euphoria' of falling in love if it meant he also avoided experiencing the disintegration of that relationship and the hatred for each other that followed.

Mac McGuire, for all she was an independent and successful artist, gave every appearance of being one of those happily-ever-after women Jonas had so far managed to avoid having any personal involvement with.

'Well?' she prompted irritably at Jonas's lengthy silence.

He should say no. Should tell this woman that he had remembered he already had a luncheon appointment today.

Damn it, it was only lunch, not a declaration of intent!

His mouth thinned. 'I have an hour free between one o'clock and two o'clock today.'

'Wow,' Mac murmured, those smoky-grey eyes now openly laughing at him. 'I should feel honoured that Jonas Buchanan feels he can spare me a whole hour of his time.'

His eyes narrowed to icy slits as he retorted, 'When what I should really do is take your shapely little bottom to court and sue you for slander!'

Mac's eyes widened and hot colour suffused her cheeks at hearing Jonas claim she had a shapely little bottom, making her once again completely aware of his own dark and dangerous attraction…

If anything he seemed even bigger today, his wide shoulders and powerful chest visibly muscled beneath the tailored suit and silk shirt, his face hard and slightly predatory, and dominated by those piercing blue eyes that seemed to see too much.

Did they see just how affected Mac was by his dark good looks, and that air of danger?

Perhaps the two of them lunching together wasn't such a good idea, after all, Mac decided with a frown. She could always claim that she had remembered a prior engagement. That she had to go to the Lyndwood Gallery to check on how the exhibition was going—

'Jonas, I have the letter here from—' The blonde, blue-eyed woman who had entered from the adjoining office, and who Mac instantly recognised as being Jonas's PA, Yvonne Richards—the same woman who had visited Mac a couple of months ago in an effort to persuade her into agreeing to sell her home—came to an abrupt halt in the doorway to Jonas's office as she saw Mac there. 'I'll come back later, shall I?' She totally ignored Mac as she looked at Jonas enquiringly.

'No need, Yvonne; Miss McGuire was just leaving,' Jonas said as he stood up, obviously dismissing Mac.

The fact that was exactly what Mac had been about to do did nothing to nullify the fact that Jonas was trying to get rid of her! Without any firm arrangements having been made for them to meet later today to continue this discussion...

'There's an Italian restaurant two streets over from this one,' she turned to inform him briskly. 'I'll book a table for us there for one o'clock.'

'Perhaps you would prefer me to book the table for the two of you?' the blonde woman offered coolly. 'Mr Buchanan's name is known to the restaurant owner,' she added pointedly as Mac looked at her enquiringly.

Mac gave the other woman a narrowed-eyed glance as

she heard the edge in her tone, recognising that Yvonne Richards, beautiful and in her late twenties, was obviously a typical case of the PA who believed herself in love with her boss. A crush that Mac doubted Jonas Buchanan was even aware of.

Mac gave the other woman a saccharin-sweet smile. 'That won't be necessary, thank you; I know Luciano personally, too.'

'Fine,' Yvonne Richards bit out before turning to her employer. 'I'll come back when you aren't so busy, Jonas.' She turned abruptly on her two-inch heels and went back into the adjoining office, the door closing sharply behind her.

Mac turned back to Jonas. 'I don't think your PA likes me!'

Jonas's mouth compressed briefly. 'She hasn't known you long enough yet to dislike you.' Before Yvonne had interrupted them Jonas had had every intention of refusing Mac's invitation to lunch, and he wasn't at all happy with the fact that, between them, Yvonne and Mac seemed to have arranged for him to have lunch at Luciano's at one o'clock today.

Mac gave an unconcerned grin, two unexpected dimples appearing in her cheeks. 'That usually takes a little longer than five minutes, hmm?'

'Precisely,' he growled.

She raised dark, mocking brows. 'Perhaps she just has a crush on you?'

An irritated scowl darkened Jonas's brow. 'Don't be ridiculous!'

Mac gave an unconcerned shrug. 'She seems—less than happy at the thought of the two of us having lunch together.'

'Will you just go away and leave me in peace, Mac?'

Once again Jonas moved to sit behind his imposing desk in obvious dismissal. 'I'll see you later,' he added pointedly as Mac made no move to respond to his less-than-subtle hint.

'One o'clock at Luciano's,' she came back mockingly before turning and walking over to the door that led out to his secretary's office.

Jonas's scowl deepened as he found he couldn't resist the temptation to look up and watch Mac leave. To be fully aware of his own response, the stirring, hardening, heated pulsing of his thighs, as he watched the provocative sway of those slender hips and pert bottom beneath fitted jeans.

She was an irritation and a nuisance, he told himself firmly. Trouble.

With a very definite capital T!

CHAPTER FOUR

'THIS is nice.'

'Is it?' Jonas asked darkly as they sat at a window table in Luciano's. It was an obvious indication that Mac was indeed known personally to the restaurateur; Jonas had dined here often enough in the past to know that Luciano only ever reserved the window tables for his best and most-liked customers.

Mac was already seated at the table, and had been supplied with some bread sticks to eat while she was waiting, by the time Jonas arrived at the restaurant at ten minutes past one. Not that he had been deliberately late; his twelve-thirty appointment had just run over time.

Everything had seemed to go wrong after she had left his office this morning. His nine-thirty appointment hadn't arrived until almost ten o'clock—which was probably as well when Jonas had spent most of the intervening time trying to dampen down his obvious arousal for Mac McGuire!

He had also found himself closely studying Yvonne throughout the morning as he searched for any signs of that 'crush' Mac had mentioned. Rightly or wrongly, Jonas didn't approve of personal relationships within the workplace—and that included unrequited ones. Which meant, if Mac was right, he would have to start looking for another PA. But if anything Yvonne's demeanour had been slightly frostier than usual, with nothing to suggest she had anything other than a working relationship with him.

Resulting in Jonas feeling annoyed with himself for doubting his own judgement, and even more irritated with Mac for mischievously giving him those doubts in the first place!

Consequently, he was feeling irritable and bad-tempered by the time he sat down at the lunch table opposite his perkily cheerful nemesis. 'Let's just order, shall we?' he grated as he picked up the menu and held it up in front of him as an indication he was not in the mood for conversation.

Mac didn't bother to look at her own menu, already knowing exactly what she was going to order: garlic prawns followed by lasagne. As far as she was concerned, Luciano made the best lasagne in London.

Instead she looked across at Jonas as he gave every indication of concentrating on choosing what he was going to have for lunch.

Every female head in the Italian bistro had turned to look at him when he'd entered a few minutes ago and taken off his long woollen coat to hang it up just inside the door. They had continued to watch him as he made his way over to the window table, several women giving Mac envious glances when he'd pulled out the chair opposite her own and sat down.

Mac had found herself watching him too; Jonas simply was the sort of man that women of all ages took a second, and probably a third, look at. He was so tall for one thing, and the leashed and elegant power of his lean and muscled body in that perfectly tailored charcoal-coloured suit was undeniable.

His irritation told her that he was also not in a good mood. 'We don't have to eat lunch together if you would rather not?' Mac prompted ruefully.

He lowered his menu enough to look across at her with icy blue eyes. 'You would rather I moved to another table? That's going to make conversation very difficult, wouldn't you say?' he taunted.

Mac felt the warmth in her cheeks at his obvious mockery. 'Very funny!'

Jonas placed his closed menu down on the table. 'I want to know more about the break-in to your studio on Saturday night. Such as how whoever it was got inside in the first place?' he asked grimly.

Mac shrugged. 'They broke a small window next to the door and reached inside to open it.'

Jonas noticed that some of the animation had left those smoky-grey eyes, presumably at his reminder of the break-in. 'You don't have an alarm system installed?'

She grimaced. 'I've never thought I needed one.'

'Obviously you were wrong,' Jonas said reprovingly.

'Obviously.' Anger sparkled in those grey eyes now. 'I have to say that I've always found people's smugness after the event to be intensely irritating!' She was still wearing the black fitted sweater and faded denims of earlier, the silky curtain of her hair framing the delicate beauty of her face to fall in an ebony shimmer over her shoulders and down her back.

Jonas relaxed back in his chair to look across at her speculatively. 'Then hopefully I've succeeded in irritating you enough to have a security system installed. Or

perhaps I should just arrange to have it done for you?'
he mused out loud, knowing it would immediately goad
her to respond with the information that he wanted.

'That won't be necessary, thank you; I have a company coming out to install one first thing tomorrow
morning,' she came back sharply. 'Along with a glazier
to replace the window that was broken.'

His eyes narrowed. 'You haven't had the glass replaced yet?'

'I just said I hadn't,' Mac bit back.

Jonas gave a disgusted sigh. 'You should have got
someone out on Sunday to fix it.'

Mac's eyes flashed darkly. 'Don't presume to tell me
what I should or shouldn't do!'

'It's a security breach—'

'Oh, give it a rest, Jonas,' she muttered wearily. 'I'm
quite capable of organising my own life, thank you.'

'I'm seriously starting to doubt that.'

'Strangely, your opinion is of little relevance to me!'
Mac snapped. 'When I suggested we have lunch to talk
about this situation I wasn't actually referring to the
break-in.'

Jonas managed to dampen down his impatience as he
smiled up at Luciano as he appeared beside their table
to personally take their order.

'I take it you don't have a date this evening?' He
mockingly changed the subject once the restaurateur
had taken note of their order and returned to his beloved
kitchen a few minutes later.

Mac knew he had to be referring to the fact that there
was garlic in both of the foods she had ordered. 'I take
it that you do?' she retorted, the Marie Rose prawns
and Dover sole he had ordered not having any garlic in
at all.

'As it happens, no.' That blue gaze met hers taunt-ingly. 'Are you offering to rectify that omission?'

Mac frowned. 'You can't be serious?'

Was he? Having spent part of the morning in un-comfortable arousal because of this woman, Jonas had once again decided that, the less he had to do with Mac the better it would be for both him and his aching erec-tion! A decision his last remark made a complete non-sense of.

'Obviously not,' he muttered.

Mac looked across at him shrewdly. 'It sounded like you were asking me out on a date.'

Jonas shrugged. 'You're entitled to your opinion, I suppose.'

'You "suppose"?' she taunted.

He scowled darkly. 'Mac, are you deliberately trying to initiate an argument with me?'

'Maybe.'

Jonas narrowed his gaze. 'Why?'

'Why not?' Mac smiled. 'It's certainly livened up the conversation!'

Jonas knew it had done a lot more than that. He was far too physically aware of this woman already; he didn't need to feel any more so. In fact, he was somewhat relieved when the waiter chose that moment to deliver their first course to them.

What the hell had he been doing, all but suggesting that Mac ask him out on a date this evening? Meeting her for lunch was bad enough, without prolonging the time he had to spend in her disturbing company. In future, Jonas decided darkly, he would just stick to taking out his usual beautiful and sophisticated blondes!

'The reviews of your exhibition in Sunday's newspa-pers were good,' he abruptly changed the subject.

She nodded. 'Your cousin was especially kind.'

'Amy is a complete professional; if she says you're good, then you're good,' Jonas said.

'I went to the gallery after seeing you this morning. It seems to be pretty busy,' Mac told him distractedly, still slightly reeling from what she was pretty sure had been an invitation on Jonas's part for them to spend the evening together too. An offer he had obviously instantly regretted making.

Which was just as well considering Mac would have had to refuse the invitation! Going to his office was one thing. Having lunch with Jonas so that they could discuss what was going on with her warehouse was also acceptable. Going out on a proper date with him was something else entirely...

In spite of the fact that Jonas Buchanan was so obviously a devastatingly attractive man, he simply wasn't Mac's type. He was far too arrogant. At least as arrogant, if not more so, as Thomas Connelly, the art critic who had considered her nothing but a trophy to parade on his arm six years ago.

She picked up her fork to deliberately spear one of the succulent prawns swimming in garlic, before raising it to her mouth and popping it between her lips. Only to glance across the table at the exact moment she did so, her cheeks heating with flaming wings of colour as she saw the intensity with which Jonas was watching the movement.

Dark and mesmerising, his eyes had become a deep and cobalt blue. There was a slight flush to his cheeks too, and those sculptured lips were slightly parted.

Mac shifted uncomfortably. 'Would you like to try one?'

That dark gaze lifted up to hers. 'What?'

She swallowed hard, feeling strangely alone with Jonas in this crowded and happily noisy restaurant. 'You seemed to be coveting my garlic prawns, so I was offering to let you try one...'

Damn it, Jonas hadn't been coveting the prawns on Mac's plate—he had been imagining lying back and having those full and red lips placed about a certain part of his anatomy as she pleasured him!

What the hell was the *matter* with him?

In the last fifteen years he had never once mixed business with pleasure. Had always kept the two firmly separate. Since meeting Mac he seemed to have done nothing else but confuse the two, with the result that he was now once again fully aroused beneath the cover of the chequered tablecloth. Hopefully there would be no reason for him to stand up in the next few minutes or his arousal would be well and truly exposed!

'No, thank you,' he refused quickly. 'I would prefer not to smell of garlic during any of my business meetings later this afternoon.'

Mac gave an unconcerned shrug of her shoulders. 'Please yourself.'

'I usually do,' Jonas said dryly.

'Lucky you,' she said.

Jonas considered Mac through narrowed lids. 'Are you saying that you don't?' he taunted. 'I thought all artists preferred to be free spirits? In relationships as well as their art?'

Mac didn't miss the contempt in his tone. Or the underlying implication that, as an artist, she probably slept around.

It would have been amusing if it weren't so obvious that Jonas had once again meant to be insulting!

Oh, Mac had lots of friends, male as well as female,

both from school and university, but that didn't mean she went to bed with any of them. That she had ever been intimately involved with anyone, in fact.

After that fiasco with Thomas, Mac had become completely focused on what she wanted to do with her life. Which was to be successful as an artist in her own right.

From the time she was twelve years old, and her art teacher had allowed her to paint with oils on canvas for the first time, Mac had known exactly what she wanted, and that was to become a successful artist first, with marriage and children second. She had become slightly sidetracked from that ambition during that brief relationship with Thomas, but if anything the realisation of his arrogance and condescension had only increased that ambition.

'If you'll excuse me, I need to go to the ladies' room.' She placed her napkin on the table before pushing back her chair and standing up.

Jonas raised dark brows. 'Was it something I said?'

Mac frowned down at him. 'That necessitates my needing to go to the ladies' room?' she drawled derisively. 'Hardly!'

Nevertheless, Jonas was left sitting alone at the table feeling less than happy, both with himself, and with his earlier biting comment. He knew very little about her personal life—the fact that he had an erection every time he was in her company really didn't count! He certainly didn't know her well enough to have deliberately cast aspersions upon the way she might choose to live her private life.

He forced himself to continue eating his own food as he waited for Mac to return.

And waited.

And waited.

After over ten minutes had passed since she'd left the table, Jonas came to the uncomfortable conclusion that she might have walked out on both him and the restaurant!

Deservedly so?

Maybe. But that didn't make the experience—the first time that a woman had ever walked out on Jonas, for any reason—any more palatable than the prawns he had just forced himself to finish eating.

He stood up abruptly to place his own napkin on the tabletop and make his way across the restaurant to the door through to the washrooms, determined to see exactly how Mac had made her escape. Only to come to a halt in the doorway and feeling completely wrong-footed as he came face to face with Mac, who was standing in the corridor in laughing conversation with one of the waitresses.

She looked at him curiously. 'Is there a problem, Jonas?'

His eyes narrowed. 'Your food is getting cold.'

'Oh, dear.' The waitress gave an apologetic smile. 'I'll talk to you later, Mac,' she said, before hurrying off in the direction of the kitchen.

Leaving Mac alone in the hallway with an obviously seriously displeased Jonas.

Well, that was just too bad!

Jonas had been deliberately insulting before she left the table, and when she'd bumped into Carla as she was leaving the ladies' room Mac had felt no hesitation in stopping to chat; Jonas Buchanan could just sit alone at the table for a few more minutes and stew as far as she was concerned.

She raised dark brows as he stepped further into the

otherwise deserted hallway and quietly closed the door behind him, enclosing the two of them in a strangely tense and otherwise deserted silence. Mac shifted uncomfortably as Jonas walked stealthily down that hallway towards her. 'I thought you said my food was getting cold?' she prompted, suddenly nervous.

'It's already cold, so a few more minutes isn't going to make any difference,' he dismissed softly.

Mac moistened dry lips as Jonas kept walking until he came to a halt standing only inches away from her. Very tall and large, his close proximity totally unnerving. 'Why do we need to be a few more minutes?' She glanced up at him uncertainly.

Jonas was enjoying turning the tables and seeing Mac's obvious discomfort—God knew she had already made his own life uncomfortable enough for one day! Since the moment he first met her, in fact. He had no doubt that leaving him sitting alone at a table in the middle of a crowded restaurant had been deliberate on her part.

A public restaurant wasn't the ideal place for what he now had in mind, either, but to hell with that—Jonas had realised in the last few seconds that he didn't just need to kiss Mac, it had become as necessary to him as breathing.

'Guess,' he murmured throatily as he stepped even closer to her.

Her eyes widened in alarm as she took several steps back until she found herself against the wall. 'Garlic breath, remember,' she reminded him hastily.

He gave an unconcerned shrug. 'That will just make you taste even better.'

'This is so not a good idea, Jonas,' she warned him desperately.

Jonas was all out of good ideas. At this precise moment he intended—needed—to go with a bad one.

His gaze held Mac's as he reached up to cup his hand against the silky smooth curve of her cheek and ran the soft pad of his thumb over her slightly parted lips, the warmth of her breath a caress against his own highly sensitised skin. An arousing caress that made his stomach muscles clench and his thighs harden.

He drew in a sharp breath as he stepped closer still and Mac instinctively lifted her hands to rest them defensively against the hardness of his chest, the warmth of those hands burning through the silk material of Jonas's shirt as he deliberately rested his body against hers.

Mac suddenly found herself trapped between the cold wall and the heat of Jonas's body, her hands crushed against his muscled chest as he slowly lowered his head with the obvious intention of kissing her.

She knew she should protest. That she should at least try to ward off this rapidly increasing intimacy.

And yet she didn't. Couldn't.

Instead her lips parted in readiness for that kiss, her breath arrested in her throat at the first heated touch of Jonas's lips against hers.

Oh, Lord...

Mac had never known anything like the sensual pleasure of having Jonas's mouth moving against hers, exploring, sipping, tasting, teeth gently biting before that kiss deepened hungrily, his body hard and insistent against hers as her hands moved up his shoulders and her fingers became entangled in the dark thickness of his hair as she pulled him even closer. Jonas pushed her against the wall and lowered his body until his arousal pressed into Mac, making her respond with an aching hotness that pooled between her thighs in a rush of moist

and fiery heat, her breasts swelling, the rosy tips hardening to full sensitivity as they pressed against the lacy
material of her bra.

Her fingers tightened in the silky softness of Jonas's
hair as that heat grew, their mouths fusing together hungrily, Mac groaning low in her throat as she felt the firm
thrust of Jonas's tongue enter her mouth. Hot, slow and
deep thrusts matched by the rhythmic movement of his
thighs into the juncture of her sensitive thighs.

Mac groaned again in pleasure as that hardness
pressed against the swollen nub nestled there, creat-
ing an aching heat deep inside her before it spread to
every part of her body, arousing her to an almost painful
degree.

God, she wanted this man with a ferocity of need she
had never imagined, never dreamt was possible. Here.
Now. She wanted to strip off their clothes and have Jonas
take her up against the wall, her legs wrapped about his
waist as he thrust deep inside her to ease that burning
ache.

As if aware of at least some of her need, Jonas moved
his hand to curve about her left breast, the soft pad of his
thumb unerringly finding the swollen tip and sweeping
across it.

Mac whimpered as the pleasure of that caress coursed
down to her thighs, and she wished Jonas could touch
her there, too—

'Well, *really*!' a shocked female voiced gasped. 'This
is a public restaurant, you know,' the woman added disgustedly as she walked past them to the washrooms.
'Why don't the two of you just get a room somewhere?'
The door to the ladies room closed behind her with a
disapproving snap.

Mac had wrenched away from Jonas the moment

she'd realised they were no longer alone in the hallway, burying the heat of her face against his chest now to hide her embarrassment at being caught in such a compromising position.

In a public restaurant, for goodness' sake!

With Jonas Buchanan, of all people.

What could she have been thinking?

She hadn't been thinking at all, that was the problem. She had been feeling. Experiencing emotions, sensations, she had never known before.

If that woman hadn't interrupted them then Mac might just have gone through with that urge she'd had to start ripping Jonas's clothes from his body before begging him to ease the burning ache between her thighs!

Oh, God.

CHAPTER FIVE

'SO, WHAT do you think?' Jonas asked as he stepped back from Mac.

'What do I think about what?' She blinked up at him as she straightened away from the wall to push the tangle of her hair back from her face; her eyes fever bright, her cheeks flushed, and those sensuously enticing lips slightly swollen from the fierce hunger of their kisses.

A hunger that had made Jonas forget, not only who they were, but *where* they were. All that had mattered to him at that moment was tasting Mac, devouring those tempting red lips, pressing the heat of his body against hers, her fingers becoming entangled in his hair as she responded to his desire.

Jonas knew he hadn't been this physically aroused, so totally lost to reason, since he was an inexperienced teenager. And he didn't like the sensation of being out of control. He didn't like it at all.

His mouth twisted. 'The two of us getting a hotel room for the afternoon.'

Mac's eyes widened. 'Certainly not!' she exclaimed indignantly.

'Why not?' he taunted.

'Why not?' Mac repeated as she glared up at him. 'I have no idea what sort of women you usually associate with, Jonas, but I can assure you that I do not go to hotel rooms with men for the afternoon!'

'I wasn't suggesting you went with men plural, Mac, just me,' he drawled.

'I said *no*!' She was breathing heavily in her agitation, the fullness of her breasts rapidly rising and falling.

Something that Jonas was all too well aware of as he looked down at her and his still heavily roused manhood pulsed achingly in response. 'You want me, I want you, so why the hell not?' he rasped.

He would have felt happier about this situation if Mac had just said yes to the two of them going to a hotel for the afternoon. That way he would have found her less of an enigma than he did now. Less intriguing than he did now.

Because Mac had definitely returned his passion. Yet it was a passion she made it clear she had no intention of doing anything about, probably not now nor in the future. He already knew his own afternoon was going to be as uncomfortable as his morning had been, but how did Mac intend dealing with her own unsatisfied arousal?

'Unless you're trying to tell me you don't want me?' he murmured.

Mac wasn't sure which of her emotions was the strongest—the urge she had to slap Jonas's arrogant face or the one she had to just sit down and cry at her own stupidity.

Because he was right, damn him. She did want him. She had never physically wanted a man more, in fact, her whole body one burning ache of need. Something Mac knew was going to bother her long after he had gone back to his office to attend his afternoon meetings.

But she definitely wanted to slap him too. For bringing

that physical awareness down to a purely basic level by suggesting they get a hotel room for the afternoon and satisfy those longings.

She really wasn't that sort of woman. She had never done anything so impulsively reckless as kissing a man so heatedly on the premises of a restaurant before, let alone gone to a hotel room with him, and she had no intention of doing the latter now with Jonas, either. Much as she might secretly ache to do so. It sounded wild. Liberating. Dangerously exciting...

She deliberately fell back on anger as the solution to her predicament. 'Whether I want you or not, an afternoon in a hotel bedroom with a man I barely know—and who I really don't want to know any better—is really not my thing,' she told him scornfully. 'If you're feeling frustrated, Jonas, then I'm sure there are any number of women you could call who would be only too happy to spend the afternoon satisfying you!'

Jonas's eyes narrowed to icy slits. 'I've never been that desperate for sex, Mac.'

Including sex with her, she knew he was implying. Which was no doubt true. Jonas was young, handsome and rich enough to attract any woman he decided he wanted. He certainly didn't need to trouble himself over one stubborn artist, who obviously irritated him as much as she aroused him.

And Mac had aroused him. She'd felt the hard evidence of that arousal pressed against her own thighs as Jonas kissed her.

Her mouth firmed. 'I suggest we just forget about lunch,' she said abruptly. 'I'm really not hungry any more, and I doubt you are either—'

'Not for food, anyway,' Jonas muttered.

'I—' Mac broke off suddenly as the woman who

had interrupted them earlier now came back out of the ladies' room, her gaze averted as she passed them and returned to the dining room of the restaurant. Mac's embarrassment returned with a vengeance. 'Don't worry, I'll explain to Luciano that you had an appointment you had to go to rather than intending any slight to the preparation of his food.'

'I moved my afternoon around. My next appointment isn't for another hour,' Jonas told her.

Her eyes widened. 'You want us to go back to the table and finish eating lunch together?'

After what just happened between us? Jonas inwardly finished Mac's question. And the answer to that was no, of course he didn't want them to return to the table and carry on eating lunch together as if nothing had happened. But neither did he appreciate Mac dismissing him as if the last few minutes had never happened at all.

His mouth thinned. 'Obviously not,' he bit out tersely. 'I'll settle the bill and explain to Luciano that *you* had a previous appointment.'

Mac frowned. 'I asked you out to lunch—'

'I'm paying the bill, Mac,' Jonas repeated firmly.

Mac continued to look up at him frowningly for several long seconds before giving an impatient shrug. 'Fine. Whatever.' Her tone implied she just wanted to get out of here. Away from him. Now.

A need she followed through on as she turned swiftly on her heel and marched down the hallway back into the restaurant, the door swinging closed behind her.

Jonas remained where he was for several more minutes after Mac had gone, eyes narrowed and his expression grim as he recognised that she was no longer just a problem on a business level, but had also become one on a personal level, too.

Perhaps one that would only be resolved once they had been to bed together…

Mac was barefooted and belatedly eating a piece of toast for her lunch when she went to answer the knock on her door later that afternoon, a brief glance through the spy-hole in the door showing her that she didn't know the grey-haired man standing at the top of the metal staircase dressed like a workman in blue overalls and a thick checked shirt. 'Yes?' she prompted politely after opening the door.

'Afternoon, love,' the middle-aged man returned with a smile. 'Bob Jenkins. I've come to replace ya window.'

Mac's brows rose. 'That's great!'

He was already inspecting the broken window next to the door. 'Had a break-in, did ya?' He gave a shake of his head. 'Too much of it about nowadays. No respect, that's the problem. Not for people or their property.'

'No.' Mac grimaced as she recalled the mess that had been left in her studio.

'It will only take a few minutes to fix.' Bob Jenkins gave her another encouraging smile. 'I'll just go and get my things from the van.'

Mac had made him a mug of tea by the time he came back up the stairs with his tools and a pane of glass that appeared to be the exact size of the one that had been broken. 'How did you know which size glass to bring?'

The glazier took a sip of tea and put the mug down before he began working on the window frame. 'The boss is pretty good at judging things like this,' he explained.

Mac sipped her own tea as she watched him work.

'Was that the man I spoke to on the telephone this morning?'

'Don't know about that, love.' Bob Jenkins looked up to give her a grin. 'He just told me to get over here toot sweet and replace the window.'

Mac had no idea why, but she had a sudden uneasy feeling about 'the boss'. Maybe because she didn't recall telling the man at the glazier company she had called this morning what size window had been broken. Or expected anyone to arrive from that company until tomorrow...

She eyed Bob warily. 'Exactly who is the boss?'

He raised grizzled grey brows. 'Mr Buchanan, of course.'

Exactly what Mac had suspected—dreaded—hearing!

After their strained parting earlier Mac hadn't expected to see or hear from Jonas ever again. Although technically, she wasn't seeing or hearing from him now, either; he had just arrogantly sent one of his workmen over to fix her broken window.

Why?

Was Jonas treating her like the 'fragile little woman' who needed the help of the 'big, strong man'?

Or was Jonas replacing the window because he knew that he—or someone who worked for him—was responsible for it being broken in the first place?

'Of course,' Mac answered the workman distractedly. 'If you'll excuse me, Bob?'

'No problem,' he assured her brightly.

Mac was so annoyed at Jonas's high-handedness that she didn't quite know what to do with all the anger bubbling inside her. What did he think he was doing, interfering in this way, when she had already told him that she had arranged for a glazier to come out tomorrow?

An arrangement he had instantly expressed his disapproval of. Enough to have arranged for one of his own workmen to come out and replace the window immediately, apparently! Were Jonas's actions prompted by a guilty conscience? Or by something else? Although quite what that something else could be Mac had no idea. It was enough, surely, that Jonas was sticking his arrogant nose into her business?

Too right it was!

'What can I do for you this time, Mac?' Jonas took his briefcase out of the car before locking it and turning to face her wearily across the private and brightly lid underground car park beneath his apartment building.

He had been vaguely aware, as he drove home at the end of what had been a damned awful day, of the black motorbike following in the traffic behind him. He simply hadn't realised that Mac was the driver of that motorbike until she followed him down into the car park, stopped the vehicle behind his car and removed the black crash helmet to shake the long length of her ebony-dark hair loose about her shoulders. The black biking leathers she was wearing fitted her as snugly as a glove, and clearly outlined the fullness of her breasts and her slender waist and hips. Jonas couldn't help thinking of how they were no doubt moulded to her perfectly shaped bottom, too!

But there was no way that Jonas could mistake the obviously hostile demeanour on her face for anything other than what it was as she climbed off the motorbike; her eyes were sparkling with challenge, the fullness of her lips compressed and unsmiling.

Jonas's afternoon had been just as uncomfortable as he had thought it might be. So much so that he hadn't been able to give his usual concentration to his business meetings.

What was it about this woman in particular that so disturbed him? Mac was beautiful, yes, but in a wild and Bohemian sort of way that had never appealed to him before. There was absolutely nothing about her that usually attracted him to a woman. She was short and dark-haired, boyishly slender apart from the fullness of her breasts, and not in the least sophisticated; she even rode a motorbike, for heaven's sake!

Jonas wasn't particularly into motorbikes, but even he recognised the machine as being a Harley, the chassis a shiny black, its silver chrome gleaming brightly. For what had to be the dozenth time, Jonas told himself that Mac McGuire was most definitely not his type.

So why the hell couldn't he stop thinking about her?

His eyes narrowed. 'Don't you think—whatever your reason for being here—that following me home is taking things to an extreme?'

Her mouth tightened further at the criticism. 'Maybe.'

He raised mocking brows. 'Only maybe?'

'Yes,' she admitted grudgingly.

He eyed her coldly. 'And so you're here because…?'

She glared at him. 'You sent a glazier to repair my window.'

'Yes.'

Her eyes widened. 'You aren't even going to attempt to deny it?'

Jonas grimaced. 'Presumably Bob told you I had sent him?'

'Yes.'

'Then what would be the point of my trying to deny it?' he reasoned impatiently.

Mac was feeling a little foolish now that she was actually face to face with Jonas. Anger had been her primary emotion, as she waited the twenty minutes or so it had taken Bob Jenkins to replace the window, before donning her leathers and getting her motorcycle out of the garage and riding it over to Jonas's office. Just in time to see Jonas driving out of the office underground car park in his dark green sports car.

Frustrated anger had made her decide to follow him home; having ridden back into the city for the sole purpose of speaking to him, Mac had had no intention of just turning round and going home without doing exactly that.

At least, she had hoped Jonas was driving home; it would be a little embarrassing for Mac to have followed him to a date with another woman!

The prestigious apartment building above this underground car park—so unlike her own rambling warehouse-conversion home—definitely looked like the sort of place Jonas would choose to live.

She stubbornly stood her ground. 'I told you I had a glazier coming out tomorrow.'

Jonas nodded tersely. 'And I seem to recall telling you that wasn't good enough.'

Her eyes widened. 'So you just arranged for one of your own workmen to come over this afternoon instead? Without even giving me the courtesy of telling me about it?'

Jonas could see that Mac was clearly running out of

steam, her accusing tone certainly lacking some of its earlier anger. He regarded her mockingly. 'So it would seem.'

'I—but—you can't just take over my life in this way, Jonas!'

He frowned. 'You see ensuring your safety as an attempt to take over your life?'

'Yes! Well…not exactly,' she allowed impatiently. 'But it was certainly an arrogant thing to do!'

Yes, she was definitely running out of steam… 'But I *am* arrogant, Mac.'

'It's not something you should be in the least proud of!'

He gave her an unapologetic, smile. 'Your objection is duly noted.'

'And dismissed!'

Jonas gave a shrug. 'I presume Bob has now replaced the broken window?'

Mac gave a disgusted snort. 'He wouldn't dare do anything else when "the boss" told him to do so "toot sweet".'

Jonas had to smile at her perfect mimicry of Bob's broad Cockney accent. 'Well, unless you want me to break the window again just so that you can have the satisfaction of having your own glazier fix it tomorrow, I don't really see what you want me to do about it.'

Those smoky-grey eyes narrowed. 'You think you're so clever, don't you?'

Jonas straightened. 'No, Mac, I think what I did was the most sensible course of action in the circumstances,' he stated calmly. 'If you disagree with that, then that's obviously your prerogative.'

'I disagree with the way you went about it, not

with the fact that you did it,' she continued in obvious frustration.

He gave a cool nod. 'Again, your objection is duly noted.'

'Right. Okay.' Mac didn't quite know what to do or say now that she'd voiced her protest over the replacement of her broken window.

She should have just telephoned Jonas and told him what she thought of him rather than coming back into town to speak to him personally. She certainly shouldn't—as he had already pointed out so mockingly—have followed him home!

The wisest thing to do now would be to get back on her motorbike and drive back home. Unwisely, Mac knew she wasn't yet ready to do that...

Just looking at Jonas, his dark hair once again ruffled by the breeze outside, the hard arrogance of his face clearly visible in the brightly lit car park, was enough to make her knees go weak. To remind her of the way he had kissed and touched her earlier today. To make her long for him to kiss and touch her in that way again.

To make her question whether that wasn't the very reason she had come here in the first place...

Jonas had been watching the different emotions flickering across Mac's expressive face. First the fading of her anger, which was replaced by confusion and uncertainty. And now he could see those emotions replaced by an unmistakable hunger in those smoky-grey eyes as she looked at him so intently...

A hunger he fully reciprocated. 'I intend to have several glasses of wine as soon as I get up to my apartment—would you care to join me?' he offered huskily.

She visibly swallowed. 'That's probably not a good idea.'

Again, here and now, Jonas was more than willing to go with a bad idea. His body physically ached from the hours he had already spent aroused by this woman today; the thought of an evening and night suffering the same discomfort did not appeal to him in the slightest. Besides, he really did want to see her perfect little bottom in those skin-tight leathers! 'Half a glass of wine isn't going to do you any harm, Mac.'

'Isn't it?'

Maybe it was, Jonas acknowledged with dark humour. If he had anything to do or say about it. 'Scared, Mac?' he taunted.

Her cheeks became flushed. 'Now you're deliberately challenging me into agreeing to go up to your apartment with you!'

He gave her an amused smile. 'Is it working?'

Mac knew that her temptation to go up to Jonas's apartment with him had very little to do with annoyance. Just talking with him like this made her nerve endings tingle, the low timbre of his voice sending little quivers of awareness up her nape and down the length of her spine, the fine hairs on her arms standing to attention, and her skin feeling as if it were covered in goose-bumps. She also felt uncomfortably hot, a heat she knew had nothing to do with the leathers she was wearing to keep out the early evening chill, and everything to do with being so physically aware of Jonas.

All of which told Mac she would be a fool to go anywhere she would be completely alone—and vulnerable to her own churning emotions—with Jonas.

Except she ached to be alone with him.

She nodded abruptly. 'I— Fine. Will it be safe to leave my helmet down here with my bike?'

'I'm sure your bike and helmet will be perfectly safe left down here,' Jonas assured her.

The implication being that it was Mac's own safety, once she was alone with him in his apartment, that she ought to be worried about.

CHAPTER SIX

MAC turned to look at Jonas as he fell into step slightly behind her as she crossed the car park to the lift that would take them up to his apartment. Only to quickly turn away again, her cheeks flaring with heated colour, as she saw the way he was unashamedly watching the gentle swaying of her hips and bottom as she walked.

He eyed her unapologetically as he stood beside her to punch in the security code that opened the lift doors and allowed the two of them to step inside. 'You shouldn't wear tight leathers if you don't want men to look at you!' He pressed the penthouse button.

Mac looked up at him reprovingly as the lift began to ascend. 'I wear them for extra safety if I should come off the bike, not for men to look at. And you know how hot *you* are on safety,' she prodded.

'Hot would seem to be the appropriate word,' Jonas teased.

Mac's cheeks felt more heated than ever at the knowledge that Jonas thought she looked hot in her biking gear. 'Perhaps we should just change the subject.'

'Perhaps we should.' He nodded, blue eyes openly laughing at her.

Mac turned away to stare fixedly at the grey metal doors until they opened onto the penthouse floor. The lights came on automatically as they stepped straight into what was obviously the sitting-room—or perhaps one of them?—of Jonas's huge apartment.

It had exactly the sort of impersonal ultra-modern décor that Mac had expected, mainly in black and white with chrome, with touches of red to alleviate the austerity. The walls were painted a cool white, with black and chrome furniture, with cushions in several shades of red on the sofa and chairs, and several black and white rugs on the highly polished black-wood floor.

Mac hated it on sight!

'Very nice,' she murmured unenthusiastically.

Jonas had seen the wince on Mac's face before she donned the mask of social politeness. 'I allowed an interior designer free rein with the décor in here when I moved in six months ago,' he admitted ruefully. 'Awful, isn't it?' He grimaced as he strode further into the room.

Mac followed slowly. 'If you don't like it, why haven't you changed it?'

He shrugged. 'I couldn't see the point when I shall be moving out again soon.'

'Oh?' She turned to look at him. 'Is that why you haven't bothered to put up any Christmas decorations, either?'

Jonas never bothered to put up Christmas decorations. What was the point? Only he lived here, with the occasional visitor, so why bother with a lot of tacky decorations that only gathered dust, before they had to be taken down again? For Jonas, Christmas was, and always had been, just a time to be suffered through, while everyone else seemed to overeat and indulge in needless sentimentality. In fact, Jonas usually made a point of disappearing to the warmth of a Caribbean island for the whole of the holidays, and, although he hadn't made any plans to do so yet, he doubted that this year would be any different from previous ones.

'No,' Jonas said shortly. Mac really did look good in those figure-hugging leathers, he acknowledged privately as once again he felt what was fast becoming a familiar hardening of his thighs. 'Come through to the kitchen and I'll open a bottle of wine,' he invited briskly before leading the way through to the adjoining room.

He had designed the kitchen himself, the cathedral-style ceiling oak-beamed using beams that had originally come from an eighteenth-century cottage, with matching oak kitchen cabinets, all the modern conveniences such as a fridge-freezer and a dishwasher hidden behind those cabinets, with a weathered oak table in the middle of the room surrounded by four chairs, and copper pots hanging conveniently beside the green Aga.

It was a warm and comfortable room as opposed to the coolly impersonal sitting-room. The kitchen was where Jonas felt most at ease, and was where he usually sat and read the newspapers or did paperwork on the evenings he was at home.

Although he wasn't too sure any more about inviting Mac McGuire into his inner sanctum...

'Much better,' she murmured approvingly. 'Did you design this yourself?'

'Yes.'

'I thought so.'

Jonas raised dark brows. 'Why?'

She gave an awkward shrug. 'It's—warmer, than the other room.'

He scowled. 'Warmer?'

'More lived-in,' she amended.

Jonas continued to look at her for several long seconds

before giving an abrupt nod. 'Make yourself comfortable,' he invited and moved to take a bottle of Chablis Premier Cru from the cooler before deftly opening it and pouring some of the delicious fruity wine into two glasses.

Mac still wasn't sure about being in Jonas's apartment at all, let alone making herself comfortable. And from the frown now on Jonas's brow she thought maybe he was regretting having invited her, too.

She sat down gingerly on one of the four chairs placed about the oak table. 'I'll just drink my half a glass of wine and then go.'

Jonas placed the glass on the table in front of her. 'What's your hurry?'

She nervously moistened her lips with the tip of her tongue as he stood far too close to her, only to immediately stop again as she saw the intensity with which Jonas was watching the movement. 'I just think it would be better if I don't overstay my welcome.' Her hand was shaking slightly as she reached out to pick up the glass and take a sip of the cool wine.

Jonas smiled slightly. 'Better for whom?'

She lifted one shoulder delicately. 'Both of us, I would have thought.'

'Maybe we're both thinking too much,' he murmured broodingly. 'Have you eaten dinner yet?'

Mac looked at him sharply. 'Not yet, no.' Surely he wasn't about to repeat his earlier suggestion that the two of them go out to dinner together?

'I only had a few prawns for lunch,' he reminded her ruefully. 'How about you?'

'I had a piece of toast when I got home. But I'm hardly dressed for going out to dinner, Jonas.'

'Who said anything about going out?' He looked at her quizzically.

Mac felt an uncomfortable surge—of what?—in her chest. Trepidation? Fear? Or anticipation? Or could it be a combination of all three of those things? Whichever it was, Mac didn't think she should stay here alone with Jonas in his apartment any longer than she absolutely had to.

'It's very kind of you to offer—'

'How polite you are all of a sudden, Mac,' Jonas cut in. 'If you don't want to have dinner with me then just have the guts to come out and say so, damn it!' His eyes glittered darkly.

She gave a pained frown. 'It isn't a question of not wanting to have dinner with you, Jonas—'

'Then what is it a question of?' he demanded harshly.

Mac swallowed hard. 'I'm not sure I belong here…'

Jonas scowled. 'What the hell does that mean?'

She gave an awkward shrug. 'I— This apartment is way out of my stratosphere. That bottle of wine you just opened probably cost what some people earn in a week.'

'And?'

'I am what I am. How I am. I hate dressing up in fancy clothes and "being seen".' She winced. 'I've already been through one experience where a man thought I would make a nice trophy to show off on his arm at parties—'

'And you think that's what I want, too?' Jonas asked.

Mac looked a little confused. 'I'm not really sure what you want from me.'

'Then that makes two of us,' Jonas told her with a

sigh. 'For some inexplicable reason you have a strange effect on me, Mary "Mac" McGuire.' His gaze held hers as he reached out and took the wine glass from her slightly trembling fingers, placing it on the table beside his own before grasping Mac's arms to pull her slowly to her feet so that she stood only inches away from him.

Jonas looked down at her searchingly, noting the almost feverish glitter in those smoky grey eyes, the flush to her cheeks, and the unevenness of her breathing through slightly parted lips. Parted lips that were begging to be kissed.

His expression was grim as he resisted that dangerous temptation. 'I'm going through to my bedroom now to change out of my suit. If you decide you don't want to stay and help me cook dinner then I suggest you leave before I get back.' He released her abruptly before turning on his heel and going out of the room in the direction of his bedroom further down the hallway.

Mac was still trembling somewhat as she stood alone in the kitchen. She should do as Jonas suggested and leave before he came back. She knew that she should. Yet she didn't want to. What she wanted to do was stay right here and spend the evening cooking dinner with him before they sat down together to eat it in this warm and comfortable kitchen…

Except she knew that Jonas wasn't suggesting they just cook and eat dinner together. Her remaining here would mean she was also agreeable to repeating their earlier shared kisses.

Mac sat down abruptly, totally undecided about what to do. She should go. But she didn't want to. She knew she shouldn't allow that explosive passion with Jonas at the restaurant to happen again. But she wanted to!

She was still sitting there pondering her dilemma

when Jonas came back into the kitchen, her breath catch-
ing in her throat as she saw him casually dressed for
the first time. The thin black cashmere sweater was
moulded to wide shoulders and the flatness of his chest
and stomach, jeans that were faded from age and wear
rather than designer-styled to be that way sat low down
on his hips and emphasised the muscled length of his
legs, and his feet were as bare as her own had been
earlier when Bob Jenkins had arrived at the warehouse
to replace her broken window. They were long and
somehow graceful feet, their very bareness seeming to
increase the intimacy of the situation.

Jonas looked everything that was tall, dark, and most
definitely dangerous!

Mac raised startled eyes. 'I decided to stay long
enough to help you cook dinner at least.'

Jonas's enigmatic expression, as he stood in the doorway, gave away none of his thoughts. 'Did you?'

She stood up quickly, already regretting that decision
as she felt the rising sexual tension in the room, her pulse
actually racing.

Even breathing was becoming difficult. 'Would you
like me to help prepare the vegetables or something?'
she offered lamely.

Jonas very much doubted that Mac wanted to hear
what he would have liked to ask her to do at this particular moment. He had never before even thought about
sitting down on one of the kitchen chairs with a woman's
naked thighs straddled either side of him as he surged
up into the heat of her, but the idea certainly had appeal
right now. Making love to Mac anywhere appealed to
him right now!

'Or something,' he murmured self-derisively as he
made himself walk across to the refrigerator and open

the door to look inside at the contents. 'I have the makings of a vegetable and chicken stir-fry if that appeals?' He looked at her enquiringly.

'That sounds fine.'

Jonas was frowning slightly as he straightened. 'Wouldn't you be more comfortable out of those leathers? Unless of course you aren't wearing anything underneath?' he added mockingly. 'In which case, neither of us is going to be comfortable once you've taken them off!'

It was time to put a stop to this right now, Mac decided. They hadn't even got as far as cooking dinner yet and already Jonas was talking about taking her clothes off!

'Of course I'm wearing something underneath,' she said, scowling at Jonas's deliberate teasing, sitting down to remove her boots before unzipping the leathers and taking them off to reveal she was wearing a long-sleeved white t-shirt and snug-fitting jeans above black socks. 'Satisfied?' she challenged as she stood up to lay her leathers over one of the kitchen chairs and place her heavy boots beside it.

'Not hardly,' Jonas murmured.

'Jonas!'

'Mac?' He raised innocent brows.

She drew in a deep, controlling breath. 'Just tell me what vegetables you want me to wash and cut up,' she muttered bad-temperedly.

'Yes, ma'am!' he shot back.

To Mac's surprise they worked quite harmoniously together as they prepared and then cooked the food, sitting down at the table to eat it not half an hour later. 'You said you'll be moving from here soon?' she reminded Jonas curiously as she looked across the table at him.

He nodded as he put his fork down on his plate and drank some of his wine before answering her. 'By this time next year we should be neighbours.'

Mac's eyes widened. 'You're moving into the apartment complex next to me once it's finished being built?'

Jonas didn't think she could have sounded any more horrified if he had said he was actually moving in with her. 'That's the plan, yes,' he confirmed dryly. 'Unless, of course, you decide to sell and move out, after all.'

Her mouth firmed. 'No, I can safely assure you that I have no intention of ever doing that.'

Jonas frowned. 'Why the hell not?'

'It's difficult to explain.'

'Try,' he invited grimly.

Mac frowned. 'The warehouse belonged to my great-grandfather originally, then to my grandfather. Years ago my great-grandfather owned a small fleet of boats, for delivering cargos to other parts of England. Obviously long before we had the huge container trucks that clog up the roads nowadays.' She chewed distractedly on her bottom lip.

Jonas's gaze was riveted on those tiny white teeth nibbling on the fullness of her bottom lip, that ache returning to his thighs as he easily imagined being the one doing the biting...

For the moment Mac seemed unaware of the heated intensity of his gaze. 'I spent a lot of time there with my grandfather when I was a child, and when he died he left it to me,' she finished with a shrug.

Jonas forced himself to drag his gaze from the sensual fullness of her lips. 'So you're saying you want to keep it because it has sentimental value?'

'Something like that, yes.'

'Your grandfather didn't want to leave the property to your parents?'

It really was difficult for Mac to explain the affinity that had existed between her grandfather and herself. How he had understood the love and affection she felt for the rambling warehouse beside the river. How living and working there now made Mac feel that she still had that connection to her grandfather. 'My parents had already moved out of London to live in Devon when my grandfather died, and so didn't want or need it.'

'No siblings for you to share with?'

'No. You?' Mac asked with interest, deciding she had probably talked about herself enough for one evening.

Jonas's mouth thinned. 'I believe my parents considered that one mistake was enough.'

Mac gasped, not quite sure what to say in answer to a statement like that. 'I'm sure they didn't think of you as a mistake—'

'Then you would be wrong, Mac,' he said dryly. 'My parents were both only nineteen when they got married, and then it was only because my mother was expecting me. She would have been better off—we all would have—if she had either got rid of the baby or settled for being a single mother.' He finished drinking the wine in his glass, offering to refill Mac's glass before refilling his own when she shook her head in refusal.

Mac had continued to eat while they talked, but she gave up all pretence of that after Jonas's comment that his mother should have got rid of him rather than marry his father!

Jonas looked bitter. 'I have no doubts that your own childhood was one of love and indulgence with parents and a family who loved you?'

'Yes,' she admitted with slight discomfort.

Jonas gave a hard smile. 'Don't look so apologetic, Mac. It's the way it should be, after all,' he said bleakly. 'Unfortunately, it so often isn't. I believe it took a couple of years for the novelty to wear off and the cracks to start appearing in my own parents' marriage, then ten years or more for them to realise they couldn't stand the sight of each other. Or me,' he added flatly.

Mac gave a pained wince. 'I'm sure you're wrong about that, Jonas.'

'I'm sure your romantic little heart wants me to be wrong about that, Mac,' he corrected.

He meant his mockery of her to wound, and it did, but Mac's 'romantic little heart' also told her that Jonas's taunts hid the pain and disillusionment that had helped to mould him into the hard and resilient man he was today. That had made him into a man who rejected all the softer emotions, such as love, in favour of making a success of his life through his own hard work and sheer determination. That had made him into a man who didn't even bother to put up Christmas decorations in his apartment...

'Your parents are divorced now?' she asked.

'Yes, thank God,' he replied. 'After years of basically ignoring each other, and me, they finally separated when I was thirteen and divorced a couple of years later.'

Mac didn't even like to think of the damage they had done in those thirteen years, not only to each other, but most especially to Jonas, the child caught in the middle of all that hostility.

'Which one did you live with after the separation?'

'Neither of them,' Jonas bit out with satisfaction. 'I had my own grandfather I went to live with. My father's father. Although I doubt Joseph was the warm and fuzzy type your own grandfather sounds,' he added.

Mac doubted it too, if Jonas had actually called his grandfather by his first name, and if the expression on Jonas's face was anything to go by!

Jonas would have found Mac's obvious dismay amusing if it weren't his own childhood they were discussing. Something that was unusual in itself when Jonas usually went out of his way not to talk about himself. But it was better that Mac knew all there was to know about him now. To be made aware that falling in love and getting married wasn't, and never would be, a part of his future. Jonas had seen firsthand the pain and disillusionment that supposed emotion caused, and he wanted no part of it. Not now or ever.

'You said earlier that you didn't belong in these surroundings,' Jonas reminded her. 'Well, neither do I. My parents were poor, and my grandfather Joseph was a rough, tough man who worked on a building site all his life. I've worked hard for what I have, Mac.'

'I didn't mean to imply—'

'Didn't you?' He gave her a grim smile. 'I probably owe part of my success to the fact that my grandfather had no time for slackers,' he continued relentlessly. 'You either worked to pay your way or you got out. I decided to work. My parents had both remarried by the time I was sixteen and disappeared off into the sunset—'

'Jonas!' Mac choked as she sat forward to place her hand over his as it lay curled into a fist on the tabletop.

He pulled his hand away sharply, determined to finish this now that he had started. Mac should know exactly what she was getting into if she decided to become involved with him. Exactly! 'In between working with my grandfather before and after school and cooking for the two of us, I also worked hard to get my A levels. Then I worked my way through university and gained a Masters degree in Mathematics before going into architecture. I worked my ba—' He broke off with an apologetic grimace. 'I worked hard for one of the best architecture companies in London for a couple of years, before I was lucky enough to have a couple of my designs taken up by a man called Joel Baxter. Have you heard of him?'

Mac's eyes were wide. 'The man who makes billions out of computer games and software?'

'That's the one,' Jonas confirmed. 'Strangely, we became friends. He convinced me I should go out on my own, that I needed to take control of the whole construction of the building and not just the design of it, that I would never make money working for someone else. It was a struggle to start with, but I took his advice, and, as they say, the rest is history.' He gave a dismissive shrug.

Yes, it was. Mac was aware of the well-publicised overnight success of Buchanan Construction—which obviously hadn't been any such thing but was simply the result of Jonas's own hard work and determination to succeed.

She moistened dry lips. 'Are you and Joel Baxter still friends?'

Jonas's expression softened slightly. 'Yeah. Joel's one of the good guys.'

Mac brightened slightly. 'And your parents, surely they must be proud of you? Of what you've achieved?'

Jonas's eyes hardened to icy chips. 'I haven't seen either one of them since my father attended my grandfather's funeral when I was nineteen.'

Mac looked at him incredulously. 'That's—that's unbelievable!'

He looked at her coldly. 'Is it?'

'Well. Yes.' She shook her head. 'Look at you now, all that you've achieved, surely—'

'I didn't say that they hadn't wanted to see me again, Mac,' Jonas cut in. 'Once Buchanan Construction became known as a multimillion-pound worldwide enterprise, they both crawled out of the woodwork to claim their only lost son,' he recalled bitterly.

Mac swallowed hard. 'And?'

'And I didn't want anything to do with either of them,' he said emotionlessly.

Mac could understand, after all that had gone before, why Jonas felt the way that he did about seeing his parents again. Understand his feelings on the subject, maybe, but accepting it, when the situation between Jonas and his parents remained unresolved, was something else. Or perhaps he considered that just not seeing or having anything to do with his parents was the solution?

She looked sad. 'They've missed out on so much.'

Jonas lifted an unconcerned shoulder. 'I suppose that depends upon your perspective.'

Mac's perspective was that Jonas's parents had obviously been too young when they married each other and had Jonas, but it in no way excused their behaviour towards him. He had been an innocent child caught up in the battleground that had become their marriage.

Was it any wonder that Jonas was so hard and cynical? That he chose to concentrate all his energies on business relationships rather than personal ones?

'Don't go wasting any of your sympathy on me, Mac,' he grated suddenly as he obviously clearly read the emotions on her face. 'You told me earlier what you didn't want, and the only reason I've told you these about myself is so that you'll know the things *I* don't want.' He paused, his mouth tightening. 'So that you understand there would be no future, no happy ever after, if you chose to have a relationship with me.'

She raised startled eyes to look searchingly across the table at Jonas as he looked back at her so intensely. She saw and recognised the raw purpose in his gaze. The underlying warmth of seduction and sensuality in those hard and unblinking blue eyes.

CHAPTER SEVEN

THE chair scraped noisily on the tiled floor as Mac suddenly stood up. 'I think it's time I was going.'

'Running scared, after all, Mac?' Jonas mocked, watching her through narrowed lids as she turned agitatedly to pick up her leathers.

She dropped the leathers back onto the chair and faced him, her chin raised challengingly. 'I'm not scared, Jonas, I just don't think I can give you what you want.'

'Oh, I think you can give me exactly what I want, Mac.' He stood up slowly to move around the table to where she stood determinedly unmoving as she looked up at him. 'Exactly what I want,' he repeated as he reached out to curve his arms about her waist and pull her firmly up against him so that she could feel the evidence of what it was he wanted from her. All that Jonas wanted from her or any woman.

Mac gasped as she felt the hardness of his arousal pressed revealingly against her. She felt an instant echoing of that arousal in her own body as heat coursed through her breasts to pool hotly between her thighs.

God, she seriously wanted this man! Wanted him so badly that she ached with it. Longed to strip the clothes from both their bodies and have him surge hard and powerfully inside her and make her forget everything else but the desire that had burned so strongly between them ever since they'd met again at her exhibition on Saturday evening.

She gave a desperate shake of her head. 'I don't do casual relationships, Jonas.'

His face remained hard and determined. 'Have you ever tried?'

She swallowed. 'No. But—' Her protest ceased the moment that Jonas's mouth claimed hers in a kiss so raw with hunger that she could only cling to the hard strength of his shoulders as she returned the heated hunger of that kiss.

Jonas felt wrapped in the luscious smell and heat that was Mac, even as his hand moved unerringly to that strip of flesh between her T-shirt and jeans that had been tantalising him all evening. He needed to know if those full breasts were bare beneath that thin cotton top, and the first touch of her creamy flesh against Jonas's fingertips made him groan low in his throat.

Mac was pure heat. Silk and sensuality as his hand moved beneath that T-shirt and up the length of her bare spine. Jonas felt the quivering vibration of her response in the depths of his body as he pressed her closer against him. He deepened the kiss, his arousal surging in response as his tongue moved skilfully across the heat of Mac's lips and then into the hot, moist vortex beneath.

She took him in, deeper, and then deeper still, as her hands moved up Jonas's shoulders to his nape, her fingers becoming entangled in the thickness of his hair as her tongue touched lightly against his, testing, questioning. Jonas instantly retreated, encouraging, enticing, giving another low groan as that hot and moist tongue shyly followed.

He stroked her satiny flesh beneath her T-shirt, closer, ever closer to the firm mounds that he now knew without a doubt were bared to his touch, loving the way Mac arched into him as his hand moved to cup and stroke one of those uptilted breasts, capturing the soft cry that escaped her lips with his mouth as his fingers grazed across the swollen nipple.

Mac had never felt this way before and felt lost to everything but Jonas as he continued to kiss and touch her, mouth devouring hers, sipping, tasting her, with deep and drugging kisses that drove her wild with longing. While his tongue brushed lightly over the sensitivity of her lips and teeth, his hand— Oh, God, what the touch of Jonas's hard and slightly calloused hand against her naked flesh was doing to her...

Her whole body felt hot, sensitised, and she gasped and writhed, the moisture flooding between her thighs as Jonas rolled her nipple between thumb and finger. Gently, and then harder, the almost pleasure-pain like nothing Mac had ever experienced before.

Her neck arched when Jonas dragged his mouth from hers, his breath hot and moist against her skin as he left a trail of kisses across her cheek, the line of her jaw, before moving down her throat to the hollows beneath, tongue dipping, tasting, as he seemed to draw in the drugging scent of her arousal with his every breath.

Mac could only cling to the power of his shoulders as he swept her along in a tidal wave of desire so strong she felt as if Jonas were her only anchor. All that mattered. Her only reality.

Jonas had never wanted a woman as much as he did Mac. Had never hungered like this before. Had never needed to be inside any woman so badly that he literally seemed to blaze with that need, every cell and nerve in his body aching for her, robbing him of his usual self-control as he longed to feel her hands on him.

His mouth moved back to claim hers in a kiss that was almost savage, Mac offering no protest as Jonas grasped the bottom of her T-shirt to tug it upwards, only breaking that kiss long enough to pull the article of clothing over her head and throw it down on the floor.

He could barely breathe, his eyes glittering darkly blue as he looked down at her tiny breasts. Their naked-ness peaked shyly through that long ebony hair. 'My God, you're beautiful,' Jonas groaned before lowering his head to capture one of those rosy red nipples into the heat of his mouth, intending to drink his fill, to wrest every last vestige of pleasure from her hot and delicious body.

Mac gasped at the first touch of Jonas's lips against her breast, her back tensing now as she arched into him, cradling his head to her as he drew her deeper, ever deeper into his mouth, tasting her sweetness, her heat, the heady smell of her arousal driving him mad with need.

He raised his head to look down at the nipple that had swollen in size, gaze intent as he turned the attention of his lips and tongue to her other breast. At the same time he released the fastening on her jeans to slip his hands beneath the material and grasp her hips before sliding further back to cup the perfectly rounded cheeks of her bottom encased in lacy panties.

Jonas looked up at Mac with darkened and hungry eyes. 'Touch me, Mac,' he growled. He deliberately, slowly, flicked his tongue against that hard and delicious nipple, watching her response as the pleasure vibrated, resonated through the whole of her body.

Mac had never felt so sensitised to the touch of

another, so aroused and needy, her body a single burning ache as she moved eagerly to return those caresses, tugging Jonas's jumper up and off his body to reveal the hard and muscled perfection of his chest before she placed her hands flat against it. He stood immobile in front of her, that glittering blue gaze hidden beneath hooded lids, but the husky exclamation of pleasure he gave as Mac touched him for the first time encouraged her, incited her to explore all of that hard, silken flesh.

He felt like steel encased in velvet, the tiny nipples hidden amongst the light covering of chest hair standing to attention as Mac ran her fingers over them delicately. She wondered curiously whether Jonas would feel the same pleasure as she did if she were to kiss him there.

'Oh, yes, Mac!' Jonas moaned at the first flick of her tongue against that tiny enticing pebble, his hand moving to curve about her nape as he threaded his fingers in the dark tangle of her hair and held her against him, encouraging, demanding.

Mac felt empowered, exhilarated with the knowledge that she could give Jonas the same pleasure he gave her, continuing to flick her tongue against him there as her hands roamed restlessly across the broad width of his back and down the muscled curve of his spine.

Mac's mouth moved down his chest as her fingers moved lightly along the length of the erection pressing against his jeans, able to feel the heat of him through the material as he grew even harder as she touched him.

Jonas stood unmoving beneath the onslaught of those caresses, barely breathing, body tense, hands clenched into fists at his sides as he fought grimly to maintain control as Mac's lips and hands drove him almost wild with need. Knowing he was losing the battle as that image he'd had earlier, of him sitting on a chair with

Mac's naked thighs wrapped about him, caused his thighs to throb and surge in painful need, his jeans too uncomfortable, too tight to contain him any longer.

'We need to be somewhere more comfortable,' he growled before he bent down and swung Mac up into his arms. He moved out of the warm kitchen, down the hallway to his bedroom, kicking the door closed behind them. He walked over to the bed and placed Mac on top of the downy duvet before turning to switch on the soft glow of the bedside light.

He stood looking down at her for several seconds, eyes dark as he looked at that cascade of straight ebony-black hair spread across his pillows, her eyes bright, cheeks flushed, lips slightly swollen from the hunger of their kisses, and then down to the swell of those perfect breasts.

Jonas drew in a harsh breath as he gazed at those orbs with their rosy-hued nipples jutting out firmly, and then down over the curving indentation of her narrow waist, a tantalising glimpse of her lacy panties visible beneath her unzipped jeans.

He sat on the side of the bed, his gaze briefly holding hers before lowering as he slowly tugged those jeans down to fully reveal those white panties with the soft curls dark behind the lace, and the long length of her legs.

Mac was barely breathing as she looked up into the dark intensity of Jonas's face as his gaze slowly, hungrily, devoured every inch of her, from her head down to her toes.

His face was flushed as that glittering blue gaze returned to meet hers. 'I'm think I'm going to have to make love to you until you beg for me to stop,' he muttered gruffly.

Mac longed for that, ached for it, but at the same time she trembled at the depth of the desire she could feel flowing between them. 'I hope you aren't going to be disappointed,' she whispered.

Those blue eyes narrowed. 'Why should I be disappointed?'

Mac shook her head. 'I'm not experienced, and—I—I don't have any protection,' she warned, not wanting to break the spell of the moment, but only too aware now of the reason Jonas's parents had married each other. Of how much he would despise any woman stupid enough to make the same mistake with him.

'You aren't on the pill?' Jonas slid open the drawer in the bedside cabinet and took out a small foil packet.

Her cheeks were flushed. 'I— No, there's never been any need.'

Jonas looked at her suspiciously as an incredulous thought suddenly occurred to him. 'You can't possibly still be a virgin?'

'Why can't I? Jonas…?' Mac frowned her uncertainty as he stood up abruptly.

Jonas stared down at her disbelievingly—accusingly— for several long seconds, before turning away to run an agitated hand through the thickness of his hair. A virgin! Jonas couldn't believe it; Mac McGuire, a beautiful woman in her late twenties, who looked and dressed like a Bohemian, was a virgin!

He turned back. 'And exactly when were you going to tell me that interesting little piece of information?' he bit out angrily. 'Or were you just going to let me find out for myself once it was too late for me to do anything about it?'

Mac gave a dazed shake of her head. 'I don't understand,' she whispered.

Jonas glared at her. 'Virgin or not, you can't be that naïve!'

Mac was too stunned by the sudden tension between them to know what to think. 'I don't believe I'm naïve at all,' she said slowly as she sat up, her hair falling forwards to cover the nakedness of her breasts. 'I thought you realised after I told you about my one youthful disaster of a relationship—Jonas, what difference does it make whether or not I've had other lovers?'

'All the difference in the world to me,' Jonas assured her harshly.

Mac gave a pained frown as she wrapped her arms defensively about the bareness of her knees. 'But *why* does it?'

'Because I have no intention of being any woman's first lover, that's why.' His jaw was tightly clenched.

'All women have a first time with someone—'

'Yours isn't going to be with me,' he reiterated.

'Most men would be only too pleased to be a woman's first lover!' Tears of humiliation glittered in her eyes as she glared back at him and she resolutely blinked them away. She refused to cry in front of him!

'Not this man,' he said fervently.

Mac couldn't believe they were having this conversation. Couldn't believe that Jonas was refusing to make love to her just because she was a virgin!

'Why is that, Jonas?' she challenged. 'Do you think that I'm making such a grand gesture because I already imagine myself in love with you? Or do you think I'm trying to trap you in some way?' Her eyes widened as she saw from the cold stiffening of Jonas's expression, the icy glitter of his eyes, that was *exactly* what he thought—and so obviously feared. 'You arrogant louse!' she scorned furiously.

'No doubt,' he acknowledged. 'But I'm sure you'll agree that it's better if this stops now?'

'Oh, don't worry, Jonas, it's stopped,' she said scathingly as she moved to sit on the side of the bed, grabbed up her jeans from the carpeted floor and started pulling them back on.

'I'm going back to the kitchen; I suggest you join me there once you've finished dressing. You might need this.' He took a black T-shirt out of the tall chest of drawers and threw it on the bed beside her before turning on his heel and leaving the bedroom, almost slamming the door behind him.

Mac stilled, unsure as to whether the tears now finally falling hotly and unchecked down her cheeks were of anger or humiliation, too confused still at the way their heated lovemaking had turned into an exchange of insults.

Did Jonas really imagine Mac was somehow trying to trap him into a relationship with her by giving him her virginity? Into making him feel responsible for her because he'd become her first lover?

If that was what he thought, what he was desperately trying to avoid, then Jonas didn't deserve her tears. He didn't deserve anything but her pity.

Unless you're in love with him, after all? a little voice deep within her wanted to know.

No. She was most definitely not. Mac had felt closer to Jonas this evening. Felt she understood him and his motivations better after hearing about his parents' marriage and his own childhood. And she had physically wanted him. That was undeniable. But none of those things added up to her being in love with him.

Not even a little bit? the same annoying voice persisted.

No, not even a little bit! she answered it firmly.

Jonas was arrogant. Cold. And his behaviour just now proved that he was also completely undeserving of her emotions or her body.

Jonas had pulled his jumper back on and was sitting at the oak kitchen table drinking some of the wine when Mac came back into the room, his gaze narrowing as he took in her appearance in his T-shirt. It was far too big for her, so long it reached almost down to her knees, the shoulder seams hanging halfway down her arms—and yet, somehow, she still managed to look sexy as hell.

Nothing at all like the virgin she was.

Jonas couldn't have known about her inexperience. He would never have guessed it from how she'd responded to him so passionately, so eagerly...

He scowled across at her broodingly. 'Having dinner together was obviously no more successful than our attempt at having lunch.' The food remained half eaten and cold on the plates.

Mac strode across the room to grab her own T-shirt from the back of the chair where Jonas had draped it. 'At least I know who to see now if I ever want to lose weight,' she retorted.

Jonas's jaw tightened. 'You're too thin already.'

Her eyes flashed a deep, smoky grey. 'I didn't hear you complaining a few minutes ago!'

He raised dark brows, his smile sardonic. 'I wasn't stating a preference now either, only fact.'

Mac wanted to slap that mocking smile off his face. No—she wanted to pummel his chest with her fists until she actually hurt him. As he had hurt her when he'd turned away from her so coldly.

She held her T-shirt protectively in front of her.

'Is there a bathroom I can use to change back into my own top?'

He kept one mocking brow raised. 'Isn't it a little late for modesty when I've already seen you naked?'

Her cheeks warmed hotly. 'Not completely!'

Jonas gave a shrug. 'The part you're going to expose, I have.'

Mac's mouth set determinedly. 'Would you just tell me where the bathroom is?'

'The nearest one is down the hallway, first door on the right,' he told her before turning away.

It was a cold and uninterested dismissal, Mac realised with a frown as she turned and walked out of the kitchen. Anyone would think that being a virgin at her age was akin to having the plague! Maybe in his eyes it was…

She wasted no time in admiring the luxurious bathroom as she quickly pulled off Jonas's overlarge T-shirt and replaced it with her own white one, a glance in the mirror over the double sink showing her that her hair was in too much of a mess for her to do any more than plait it loosely in an effort to smooth it into some sort of order.

Her face was very pale, her eyes huge and slightly red from the tears she had shed earlier, her lips full and swollen from the intensity of the kisses she had shared with Jonas.

Most of all she looked…sad.

Which wouldn't do at all, Mac decided as she set her shoulders determinedly before leaving the bathroom to go back to the kitchen. She was a mature and confident woman—even if, horror or horrors, she was still a virgin!—and she intended to act like one.

Jonas was still sitting at the table surrounded by the

remains of their meal, although the level of wine in his glass had definitely gone down in her absence.

Mac placed his T-shirt on the back of one of the other chairs. 'Thank you,' she said stiltedly, her face averted as she sat down to begin pulling on her leathers.

This, putting her clothes back on in a strained and awkward silence, had to be one of the most embarrassing and humiliating experiences of her entire life. More embarrassing than if she and Jonas had actually made love completely? Probably not, she acknowledged with a self-derisive grimace, as she could only imagine his reaction if he had discovered her virginity when it was too late for him to pull back.

Once again Jonas watched Mac broodingly through narrowed lids, easily able to read the self-disgust in her expression, the underlying hurt. Damn it, he had never meant to hurt her. Hadn't wanted to hurt her. He just knew he had nothing to offer a woman like Mac. Beautiful. Emotional. Virginal…

His relationships were always, *always* based on a mutual attraction and physical need. That desire definitely existed between himself and Mac, but the fact that she was still a virgin, and had been willing to give that virginity to him, had also warned him that if they made love together then she would probably want more from him than that. Much more.

Jonas didn't have any more than that to give. Not to Mac or any other woman. But that wasn't her fault.

'I'm sorry.'

She gave him a sharp glance as she straightened from lacing her boots. 'For what?'

Jonas grimaced. 'For allowing things to go as far between us just now as they did. If I had known—'

'If you had known I was a virgin then you wouldn't

have invited me up to your apartment at all!' she finished knowingly as she stood to zip up her leathers.

Jonas winced at the bitterness he could hear in her tone. 'None of what happened was premeditated on my part—'

'No?' she challenged.

'No, damn it!' A scowl darkened his brow.

Mac shrugged. 'Don't worry about it, Jonas. Not all men are as fickle as you; I'm pretty sure I can find one who's more than willing to become my first lover. Maybe I'll come back once I have, and we can finish what we started?' she taunted.

Jonas pushed his chair back noisily to stand up. 'Don't be so stupid!' he rasped harshly.

Mac's chin tilted with determination as she looked up at him. 'What's stupid about it?'

'You can't just decide to lose your virginity in that cold-blooded way!'

'Why can't I?'

He shook his head. 'Because it's something too precious to just throw away. It's a gift you should give to a man you care about. That you love.'

Mac felt a clenching in her chest as she acknowledged that she *did* care about Jonas. She didn't think she was in love with him yet—it would be madness on her part to fall in love with him!—but she definitely cared about him. About the hurt child he had once been, and the disillusioned man he now was.

She looked him straight in the eye. 'I believe that's for me to decide, Jonas, not you.'

'But—'

'I would like to leave now,' she told him flatly.

Jonas stared down at her in obvious frustration. 'Not

until you promise me that you aren't going to leave here and do something totally reckless.'

'Like taking a lover?'

'Exactly!'

Mac gave him a pitying glance. 'I don't believe that anything I do in future is any of your business.'

His mouth was set grimly, a nerve pulsing in his tightly clenched jaw. 'If you're really that desperate for a lover—'

'Oh, I'm not desperate, Jonas,' she said coolly. 'Just curious,' she added, deliberately baiting him.

Jonas wanted to shake her. Wanted to grasp the tops of Mac's arms and shake her until her teeth rattled. Except that he didn't dare touch her again. Because he knew that if he did, he wouldn't be able to stop...

He sighed heavily. 'I thought you understood after the things I told you about my childhood. Mac, I'm not the man you need, and I never could be.'

She frowned. 'I don't believe I ever asked you to be anything to me,' she pointed out.

'But you would.' That nerve continued to pulse in his jaw. 'Perhaps you would enjoy the novelty of the relationship at first, the sexual excitement, but eventually you would want more than I have to give you.'

'You know what, Jonas,' she said conversationally, 'I think you're taking an awful lot for granted in assuming that I would have wanted to continue a—a sexual relationship with you after tonight. I mean, who's to say I would actually have enjoyed having sex with you? Or is it that you're under the illusion you're such a great lover that no woman could possibly be left feeling disappointed after sharing your bed?'

Jonas felt the twitch of a smile on his lips as Mac deliberately insulted him. 'That would be a little arrogant of me, wouldn't it?'

'More than a little, I would have said,' she shot back. 'So, how do I get out of here?' She moved pointedly across the room to stand beside the doorway out into the hallway.

This evening had been something of another disaster as far as he and Mac were concerned, Jonas acknowledged ruefully as he preceded her out of the kitchen and walked with her to the lift.

She grimaced once she had stepped inside the lift. 'I'm not sure if I said this before, but thank you for sending Bob over this afternoon to fix my window.'

Jonas had totally forgotten that was the original reason she had followed him home! 'But don't do anything like it again?' he guessed dryly.

'No.'

He nodded. 'That's what I thought. I—If I don't see you again before then—Merry Christmas, Mac.'

She eyed him quizzically. 'And I'd already marked you down as the "bah, humbug" type!'

'I am the "bah, humbug" type,' he admitted with a quirk of his mouth.

Mac nodded as the lift doors began to close. 'Merry Christmas, Jonas.'

Jonas continued to stand in the hallway long after she had gone down to the car park and no doubt driven away on that powerful motorbike as if the devil himself were at her heels.

He liked Mac, Jonas realised frowningly. Liked the way she looked. Her spirit. Her independence. Her optimism about life and people in general. Most of all he admired her ability to laugh at herself.

Unfortunately, he also knew that allowing himself

to like Mac McGuire was as dangerous to the solitary
lifestyle he preferred as having a sexual relationship
with her would have been.

CHAPTER EIGHT

IT WAS late in the morning when Mac parked her four-wheel-drive Jeep next to her motorbike in the garage on the ground floor of the warehouse after arriving back from a three-day pre-Christmas visit to her parents' home in Devon.

She had felt the need to get away for a while after the disastrous and humiliating end to the evening spent with Jonas at his apartment. And as the men had duly arrived the following day to install the alarm system to the warehouse, and the exhibition at the gallery was going well—Jeremy had informed Mac when she spoke to him on the telephone that the paintings were all sold, and the public were pouring in to see them before the exhibition came to a close at Christmas—she was free to do what she wanted for the next few days, at least.

Just as she had hoped, the time spent with her parents—the normality of being teased by her father and going Christmas shopping with her mother—had been the perfect way to put things in her own life back into perspective. For her to decide that her behaviour that evening at Jonas's apartment had been an aberration. A madness she didn't intend ever to repeat. In fact, she had come to the conclusion that ever seeing Jonas Buchanan again would be a mistake...

Which was going to be a little hard for her to do when he was the first person she saw as she rounded the corner from the garage!

Mac's hand tightened about the handle of the holdall she had used to pack the necessary clothing needed for her three days away, her gaze fixed on Jonas as she walked slowly towards him. She unconsciously registered how attractive he looked in a brown leather jacket over a tan-coloured sweater and faded jeans...

Any embarrassment she might have felt at seeing him again was forgotten as she realised he was directing the actions of the two other men, workmen from their clothing, who seemed to be in the process of building a metal tower beside the warehouse. 'What on earth are you doing?' Mac demanded.

'Oh, hell!' Jonas muttered as he turned and saw her, his expression becoming grim. 'I'd hoped to have dealt with this before you got back.'

'Hoped to have dealt with *what*? What on earth...?' Mac stared up at the wooden sides of the warehouse. Her eyes were wide with shock as she took in the electric-pink and fluorescent-green paints that had been sprayed haphazardly over the dark wooden cladding.

'It isn't as bad as it looks...'

'Isn't it?' she questioned sharply, the holdall slipping unnoticed from her fingers as she continued to stare numbly up at that mad kaleidoscope of colour.

'Mac—'

'Don't touch me!' She cringed away as Jonas would have reached out and grasped her arm. 'Who—? Why—?' She gave a dazed shake of her head. 'When did this happen?'

'I have no idea,' Jonas rasped. 'Some time yesterday evening, we think—'

'Who is *we*?'

'My foreman from the building site next door,' he elaborated. 'He noticed it this morning, and when he didn't receive any reply to his knock on your door he decided to report it to me.'

Mac swallowed hard, feeling slightly nauseous at the thought of someone deliberately vandalising her property. 'Why would anyone do something like this?'

'I don't know.' Jonas sighed heavily.

'Could it be kids this time?'

'Again, I have no idea. These two men are going to paint over it. They should be finished by this evening.' He grimaced. 'I had hoped to have had it done before you got back—'

'I thought I had made it plain the last time we met that I would rather you didn't go around arranging things for me?' Mac reminded him coldly.

Jonas eyed her with a frown, the pallor of her cheeks very noticeable against the red padded body-warmer she wore over a black sweater and black denims. He didn't like seeing the glitter of tears in those smoky-grey eyes, either. But he liked the cold, flat tone of her voice when she spoke to him even less. 'Would you rather I had just left it for you to find when you got home?'

'I have found it when I got home!' Her voice rose slightly, almost shrilly.

Jonas shook his head. 'I wasn't expecting you to be back just yet; I had hoped it would be later today, or even better, tomorrow morning.'

Those huge grey eyes settled on him suspiciously. 'How did you even know I had gone away?'

Jonas knew he could have lied, prevaricated even, but the suspicion he could read in Mac's expression warned him not to do either of those things. 'The Patels,' he revealed unapologetically. 'Once I had seen the mess, and you obviously weren't at home, I went to their convenience store and asked if they had any idea where you were.'

Those misty grey eyes widened. 'And they just told you I had gone away for a few days?'

He gave a rueful nod. 'Once I'd explained about the vandalism, yes.'

'Tarun always puts a daily newspaper by for me,' Mac muttered absently. 'I cancelled it while I was away.'

Jonas smiled. 'So he told me.'

She sighed and ran a hand through her hair. 'Nothing like this ever happened before I met you—'

'Don't say something you'll only have to apologise for later,' Jonas warned through suddenly gritted teeth.

'Even before,' Mac continued as if he hadn't spoken, 'when your assorted employees came here to try and persuade me into selling the warehouse, nothing like this happened. It's only since actually meeting *you*—'

'I said stop, Mac!' A nerve pulsed in his tightly clenched cheek.

Her gaze narrowed as she focused on him. 'Since meeting you, I've had my window broken and my home vandalised,' she said accusingly. 'And now some helpful soul has decided to redecorate the outside of the warehouse for me. Bit too much of a coincidence, don't you think, Jonas?' Her eyes glittered with anger now rather than tears.

Jonas had known exactly where Mac was going with this conversation, and had tried to stop her from actually voicing those accusations.

Damn it, he had considered himself well rid of her once she'd left his apartment on Monday evening. He'd had no intention of going near her on a personal level ever again if he could avoid it. Unfortunately, he hadn't been able to avoid coming here, at least, once he'd received the telephone call earlier this morning from his foreman.

He certainly wasn't enjoying being the object of Mac's suspicions. 'Only if you choose to look at it that way,' he bit out icily.

She eyed him challengingly. 'Did you report this to the police?'

Jonas narrowed cold blue eyes. 'I have the distinct feeling that I'm going to be damned if I did, and damned if I didn't.'

Mac raised questioning brows. 'How so?'

'If I did report it then I was probably just covering my own back. If I didn't report it, then again, I'm obviously guilty.'

Mac was feeling sick now that the shock was fading and reaction was setting in. She didn't want Jonas to be in any way involved in this second act of vandalism. It was the last thing she wanted! It was only that the coincidence of it all was so undeniable...

She closed her eyes briefly before opening them again. 'Your men seem to have everything well in hand,' she acknowledged ruefully as she glanced up at the two men now scaling the metal tower with the familiarity of monkeys, pots of paint and brushes in their hands. 'Would you like to come upstairs for some coffee?'

Jonas raised surprised brows. 'Are you sure it's wise to invite the enemy into your camp?'

Mac straightened from picking up the holdall she had dropped minutes ago. 'Have you never heard the saying "keep your friends close, but your enemies even closer"?' she teased.

His mouth tightened. 'I'm not your enemy, Mac.'

'I wasn't being serious, Jonas,' she assured him wearily.

'Strange, I didn't find it in the least funny,' he muttered as he began to follow her up the metal staircase.

Those psychedelic swirls of paint were even more noticeable from the top of the staircase, evidence that the perpetrator had probably stood on the top step in order to spray onto the second and third floor of the building. They had certainly made a mess of the stained dark wood.

But why had they?

Was it just an act of vandalism by kids thinking they were being clever? Or was it something else, something more sinister?

Mac gave a disgruntled snort as she unlocked the door and entered the living area of the warehouse, dropping her holdall just inside the door before going over to the kitchen area to prepare the pot of filtered coffee.

She was so lost in thought that she didn't notice for several seconds that Jonas had closed the door behind him and come to a complete halt. She eyed him curiously. 'Is there something wrong?'

Jonas was completely stunned by the inside of Mac's warehouse. He had never seen anything like this before. It was—

'Jonas?'

He blinked before focusing on Mac as she looked across at him in puzzlement. 'I—' He shook his head. 'This is—'

'Weird?' she finished dryly as she stepped out from behind the breakfast bar that partitioned off the kitchen area from the rest of the living space. 'Odd? Peculiar? A nightmare?' she concluded laughingly.

'I was going to say *fantastic*!' Jonas breathed incredulously as he now looked up at the high ceiling painted like a night sky, with the moon and stars shimmering mysteriously in that darkness.

The rest of the living area was open plan, the four walls painted like the seasons; spring was a blaze of yellow flowers against burgeoning green, summer a deeper green and gorgeous range of rainbow colours, autumn covered the spectrum from gold to russet, and winter was a beautiful white landscape.

The furniture was a mixture of all those colours, one chair gold, and another terracotta, the sofa burnt orange, with several white rugs on the highly polished wooden floor, that flat-screen television Mac had once mentioned tucked away in a corner. The bedroom area was slightly raised and reached by three wooden steps, the cover over the bed a patchwork of colours, a spiral staircase in another corner of the room obviously going up to the studio above.

And in place of honour in front of the huge picture window was a real pine Christmas tree that reached from floor to ceiling, and was decorated with so many baubles it was almost impossible to see the lushness of the branches.

Jonas had never seen anything so unusual—or so beautiful—as Mac's warehouse home. Much as Mac herself was unusual and beautiful? he wondered…

He firmly closed off that avenue of thought as he turned to give her a rueful smile. 'No wonder you didn't like the décor in the sitting-room of my apartment.'

Mac brought over two mugs of coffee and put one of them down on the low bamboo tabletop before carrying her own over to sit down on the sofa, her denim-covered legs neatly tucked beneath her. 'Obviously I prefer to go with the rustic look!' she teased, sipping her coffee.

Jonas picked up the second mug and sat down in the terracotta-coloured chair facing her. 'Is the studio upstairs like this, too?'

'I'll show it to you, if you like.'

Jonas eyed Mac curiously as he sensed the reluctance behind her offer. 'You don't usually show people your studio, do you?' he guessed.

She grimaced. 'Not usually, no.'

And yet she was offering to show it to *him*...

Jonas wasn't sure if he felt privileged or alarmed at the concession, but his curiosity was such that he wanted to see the studio anyway. 'Perhaps after we've drunk our coffee,' he suggested lightly.

'Perhaps,' Mac echoed uneasily, not altogether sure what to do with Jonas now that he was here.

She had only invited him in for coffee because their earlier conversation had been deteriorating into accusations on her part and defensive warnings on Jonas's. But now that he was here, in the intimacy of her home, she was once again aware of that rising sexual tension between them that never seemed to be far from the surface whenever the two of them were together.

Jonas looked very fit and masculine in his casual clothes, and that overlong dark hair was once again slightly ruffled by the cold wind blowing outside, his face as hard and sculptured as a statue Mac had once seen depicting the Archangel Gabriel. As for those fathomless blue eyes...

She turned away abruptly. 'You never did tell me whether or not you had informed the police about this second incident of vandalism in just a few days?'

His mouth tightened. 'I did call them, yes. Two of them arrived about an hour ago and looked the place over. If I understood them correctly, they were of the opinion that the demolishing of the other warehouses around this one has left it rather exposed and so a prime target for bored teenagers wanting to cause mischief.'

Mac was pretty sure that he had understood the police correctly. 'And what's *your* opinion, Jonas?'

His eyes narrowed. 'I think it's more—personal, than that.'

She gave a rueful smile. 'We aren't back to that disgruntled ex-lover theory again, are we?' she said dryly.

Hardly, when Jonas now knew only too well that there had never been a lover in Mac's life, ex or otherwise! Not even the man who had wanted her to be a trophy on his arm to show off at parties...

He gave a tight smile. 'I prefer to go with the jealous rival theory.'

'We've only been out together once,' she taunted. 'And that was something of a disaster, if you remember? I doubt that would have made any of your other...*women friends* jealous of me.'

Unfortunately, Jonas remembered every minute he had ever spent in this woman's company. 'Very funny.' He scowled. 'I was actually referring to a professional rival of yours rather than a personal angle involving me.'

'That would make sense seeing as we don't have a *personal* relationship—from any angle,' she said cuttingly.

Jonas deliberately chose not to enter into any sort of argument as to what there was or wasn't between himself and Mac. 'I understand your exhibition has been a tremendous success—'

'Understand from whom?' Mac pounced on his comment.

'Mac, you were the one who asked for my opinion, so would you now just let me finish giving it instead of jumping down my throat after every sentence?' he snapped his frustration with her interruptions.

'Fine,' she sighed.

'Is there anyone you know, or can think of, who might be—less than happy, shall we say, at the success of your exhibition?'

'No, there isn't,' she answered snippily. Emphatically.

Which brought Jonas back to that frustrated exboyfriend again...

He looked at her through narrowed lids. 'Where have you been for the past three days?'

She looked startled. 'Sorry?'

'I asked where you've been for the past three days,' Jonas repeated firmly.

Mac gave an irritated frown. 'I can't see how that's any of your business!'

'It is if it has any bearing on the unwanted graffiti outside,' he reasoned.

'I don't see how it can have.' Mac sat forward and put her empty coffee mug down on the bamboo table. 'If you must know, I went to visit my parents in Devon,' she explained as Jonas continued to look at her questioningly.

'Oh.' He looked frustrated. 'As you said, that's not particularly helpful.'

It also wasn't the answer he had obviously been expecting. 'Where did you think I'd been, Jonas?' Mac asked.

'How the hell should I know?' he retorted tersely.

Was he being defensive? It certainly sounded that way to her. But why did it? Jonas had made it more than clear on Monday evening that he wasn't interested in becoming involved with her—or indeed with any woman who was so physically inexperienced!

Thinking about what had happened between the two of them that evening perhaps wasn't the right thing for her to do when they were sitting here alone in her home. Well…alone apart from the two men she could see outside the window painting the wooden cladding!

She stood up suddenly. 'I don't think we'll achieve anything further by talking about this any more today, Jonas.'

He looked up at her mockingly. 'Is that my cue to politely take my leave?'

Mac felt the warmth of the colour that entered her cheeks. 'Or impolitely, if you would prefer,' she said sweetly.

What Jonas would *prefer* to do was something he dared not allow himself.

The last few minutes spent here with her, in the warmth and beauty that she had made of her home, made him strangely reluctant to leave it. Or her. Just the thought of going back alone to the cold and impersonal sterility of his own apartment was enough to send an icy shiver of revulsion down the length of his spine.

What was it about this woman in particular that made Jonas want to remain in her company? That made him so reluctant to leave the warmth and vitality that was Mary 'Mac' McGuire?

'Have you ever done any interior designing other than your own?' he heard himself asking.

Mac raised an eyebrow. 'Not really. A room here and there for my parents, but otherwise no. Why?'

What the hell was he doing? Jonas wondered, annoyed with himself. The last thing he wanted—the *very* last thing—when he moved into his new apartment next year was a constant reminder of this unusual woman because he was surrounded by *her* choice of décor!

'No reason,' he replied coldly as he stood up decisively. 'I was just making conversation,' he explained. 'You're right, I have to get back to the office.'

Mac stood near the door and watched beneath lowered lashes as Jonas strode over to place his empty coffee mug on the breakfast bar, her gaze hungry as she admired the way his brown leather jacket fitted smoothly over the width of those shoulders and how his legs appeared so long and lean in his snug faded jeans.

She wasn't over him!

Mac had thought—and hoped—that three days in Devon would put this man and that mad desire she had felt for him on Monday evening into perspective. Looking at him now, feeling the wild beat of her pulse and the heated awareness washing over her body, she realised that all she had done was force herself not to think about him. Being with Jonas again, and once more totally aware of that unequivocally passionate response to him, showed her that she hadn't forgotten a thing about him since she'd last seen him.

She moistened dry lips, instantly aware of her mistake as she saw the way Jonas's dark gaze fixated on the movement as he walked slowly towards her. 'I really do need to go out and get some things in for dinner,' she said desperately.

Jonas came to a halt only inches away from her. 'Why don't I take you out to dinner this evening and you can do the food shopping tomorrow?' he prompted huskily.

Mac blinked her uncertainty, part of her wanting to

have dinner with him this evening, another part of her knowing it would be reckless for her to even think of doing so. 'I thought we had already agreed that the two of us seeing each other again socially was not a good idea?'

'It isn't,' Jonas acknowledged wryly.

'Then—'

'I want to have dinner with you, damn it!' he bit out fiercely.

Mac gave a rueful smile. 'And do you usually get what you want, Jonas?'

'Generally? Yes. As far as you're concerned? Rarely,' he said bluntly.

Mac was torn. An evening spent alone, after being with Jonas again, now stretched in front of her like a long dark tunnel. Alternately, spending any part of the evening with him presented a high risk of there being a repeat of Monday evening's disaster...

'No,' she said finally. 'I—no.'

Jonas eyed her speculatively. 'That's a definite no, is it?'

'Yes.'

'Yes, that's a definite no? Or yes, I've changed my mind and would love to have dinner with you this evening, Jonas?' he drawled.

He was teasing her! It was so unexpected from this normally forcefully arrogant man that Mac couldn't stop herself from laughing softly as she gave a slight shake of her head. 'You aren't making this easy for me, are you?'

Jonas had no idea what had possessed him to make the invitation in the first place, let alone try to cajole her into accepting it. Especially when he knew that spending

any more time with this woman was the very last thing
he should do.

He had been telling himself exactly that for the past
three days. To no avail, obviously, when the first time he
set eyes on her again he was pressing her to have dinner
with him!

Even now Jonas couldn't bring himself to retract the
invitation. 'It can't be that difficult, Mac,' he cajoled.
'The answer is either yes or no.'

Mac looked up at Jonas quizzically, wondering why
he had invited her out to dinner when he was so obviously as reluctant to spend time alone with her again as
she was with him.

Except the two of them were alone right now...

Alone, and with the sexual tension between them
rising just as obviously. The very air that surrounded
them seemed to crackle with that awareness; she was
so aware of it now that her heart raced and her palms
felt damp.

She drew in a sharp breath. 'I think that has to be a
definite no.'

'"I think" is surely contradictory to "definite"?' Jonas
pressed.

Because Mac was having a problem *thinking* at all
in Jonas's company!

Because she really wanted to say yes?

Maybe. No, definitely! But the part of her that
could still reason logically—a very small part of her,
admittedly!—knew it really wasn't a sensible thing for
her to spend any more time in his highly disturbing
company.

'I don't want to go out to dinner with you, Jonas,' she
stated very firmly—at the same time aware of a sinking
disappointment in the pit of her stomach. An ache. A

hollowness that instantly made her want to retract her refusal. She bit her bottom lip, hard, to stop herself from doing exactly that.

Jonas looked down at Mac through narrowed lids, physically aware of everything about her; the slender and sexy elegance of her body, the long silky length of her ebony hair, the warm grey of her eyes, her tiny up tilted nose, the satiny smoothness of her cheeks, those full and sensuous lips—the bottom one firmly gripped between her tiny white teeth. Could that be in an effort to stop Mac from retracting her own refusal?

Implying she didn't *really* want to say no to his dinner invitation...

Jonas straightened. 'I'm not asking you out so that you can dress up and be a trophy on my arm, Mac,' he assured her gently. 'How about we eat here instead of going out? I'll come back at eight o'clock with a bottle of wine and a takeaway. Would you prefer Chinese or Indian?'

Mac's eyes widened. 'But I just said—'

'That you didn't want to go out to dinner,' he cut in. 'So we'll eat dinner here instead.'

She frowned. 'That wasn't quite what I meant.'

'I know that, Mac.' Jonas smiled.

'Then—'

'Look, we both know that we would actually prefer not to spend any more time together,' Jonas said neutrally. 'The problem with that is I can't seem to stay away from you. How about you?' he asked, eyes suddenly fierce with emotion in his otherwise calm face.

Mac realised from his careful tone and fierce expression that he disliked intensely even having to make that admission. That he was still as disturbed by their physical attraction to each other as she was. A physical attraction that was going precisely nowhere when he distrusted her sexual inexperience and she distrusted her own ability to resist him. To see him any more than was absolutely necessary would be absolute madness.

She drew herself up determinedly. 'I said no, Jonas, and I meant *no*!'

His mouth tightened, jaw clenched. 'Fine,' he said tersely. 'I'll wish you a pleasant evening, then.' He nodded abruptly before crossing to the door, closing it softly behind him as he left.

That hollow feeling deepened in Mac's stomach as she watched him go. She knew absolutely that the last thing she was going to have was a pleasant evening in any shape or form.

CHAPTER NINE

'I HAVE Miss McGuire for you on line one, Mr Buchanan,' Mandy informed Jonas lightly down the telephone line when he responded to her buzz.

'Miss McGuire?' Jonas frowned as he suddenly realised Mandy was referring to Mac; he had ceased thinking of her as 'the irritating Miss McGuire' days ago!

He and Mac had only parted a few hours ago, and not exactly harmoniously, so why was she calling him at his office now? Had something else happened at her home?

Jonas put his hand over the mouthpiece to look across at Yvonne as she sat on the other side of his desk, the two of them having been going through some paperwork. 'Would you come back in fifteen minutes so we can finish up here?'

'Of course, Jonas.' She stood up smoothly. 'Are you having better luck persuading Miss McGuire into selling?' she paused to ask ruefully.

Jonas gave her an irritated look. 'It hasn't come into our conversation for some time,' he answered honestly. Part of him had forgotten why he had ever met Mac in the first place. Part of him wished that he never had.

'Oh.' Yvonne looked surprised. 'I thought that was the whole point of your—acquaintance?'

'Did you?' Jonas returned unhelpfully. Yvonne was a good PA, a damned good one, but even so that didn't give her the right to question any of his actions. 'If you wouldn't mind, this is a private call…?' he prompted pointedly, regretting the embarrassed colour that entered Yvonne's cheeks, but making no attempt at an apology as he waited for her to leave his office before taking Mac's call. 'Yes?' he said tersely, not sure who he was annoyed with, only knowing that he was.

Mac had been aware of each second she'd been kept waiting to be put through to Jonas—perhaps because he was unsure about taking her call?—and she could hear the displeasure in his voice now as she held her mobile to her ear with one hand and poured two mugs of coffee with the other. 'Have I called at a bad time?'

'No.'

Mac begged to differ, considering that long wait, and the impatience she could hear in Jonas's tone. She knew she shouldn't have telephoned him. Had tried to talk herself out of it. Wished now that she had heeded her own advice! 'I realised after you had left earlier that I hadn't… I just called to say thank you,' she said awkwardly. 'For everything you did for me this morning. Calling the police. Arranging to have the graffiti painted over.'

There was a brief silence before Jonas answered, his voice sounding less aggressive. 'Have Ben and Jerry finished the painting now?'

'Ben and Jerry? That's what they're called?'

'Yes,' Jonas answered dryly.

'Really?'

'Yes, really,' Jonas chuckled softly.

Mac felt slightly heartened by that chuckle. 'They've

almost finished, yes. I was just making them both a mug of coffee.'

'That's very…kind of you.'

Mac bristled. 'You sound surprised?'

His sigh was audible. 'Let's try to not have another argument, hmm, Mac.'

'No, of course not.' She grimaced. 'Sorry.'

'Was that the only reason you called?' Jonas asked huskily.

Was it? Mac had convinced herself that it was before she made the call, but now that she had heard his voice again she wasn't so sure.

They had parted with such finality earlier. Leaving no room for manoeuvre. Something that had left Mac with a feeling of uneasy dissatisfaction.

'I think so,' she answered.

'But you're not sure?' he pressed.

'I am sure,' she said firmly. 'I just— Anyway, thank you for your help earlier, Jonas. It is appreciated.'

'You're welcome,' he said warmly. 'Have you had second thoughts about dinner?'

Second and third ones, Mac acknowledged ruefully. But all of them with the same conclusion—that a relationship between herself and Jonas was going nowhere. Except possibly to a broken heart on her part.

She wasn't sure when—or even how—the feelings she had for Jonas had sneaked up on her. She only knew that they had.

Quite what those feelings were, she had so far shied away from analysing; she only knew, after seeing him again this morning, that her three days away had achieved nothing and that she definitely felt something for him.

She felt energised in his company. A tingling awareness. An excited thrumming. Whether or not that was just a sexual excitement, Mac wasn't experienced enough in relationships to know. She only knew that the thought of never seeing him again, speaking to him again, was a painful one.

It made no difference to those feelings whatsoever that she knew there was no future for the two of them. Jonas undisputedly affected her in a way no other man ever had.

'I'll take it from your delay in answering that you have,' he drawled softly.

'I didn't say that—'

'In which case, Indian or Chinese?' he said authoritatively, rolling right over her vacillation, having no intention of letting her wriggle out of the invitation a second time. Or was it a third time? Whatever. For some reason, Mac had called him, once again opening the line of communication between them, and at the same time renewing Jonas's own determination to see her again. 'I'm waiting, Mac,' he added.

Her raggedly indrawn breath was audible. 'Indian. But—'

'No buts,' Jonas cut in forcefully. 'I'll be there about eight o'clock, okay?'

'I—Yes. Okay.'

Jonas only realised he had been tensed for another refusal as he felt his shoulders relax. 'We're only going to eat dinner together, Mac,' he mocked gruffly—not sure whether he was offering her that reassurance or himself!

Himself, probably, he accepted derisively. Mac had got under his skin in a way he wasn't comfortable with. So much so that he knew he shouldn't see her again. So much so that he knew he *had* to see her again.

She was a magnet he was inexorably drawn to. And resistance on Jonas's part was proving as futile as preventing the proverbial moth from being drawn to a flame...

'Very festive,' Jonas told Mac dryly later that evening once she had opened the door to his knock and he had stepped into the living area of the warehouse, the main lights switched off to allow for the full effect of the brightly lit Christmas tree. The smell of pine was thick in the air, and the branches were heavily adorned with decorations and glittering shiny baubles that reflected those coloured lights.

The dining table in the corner of the huge open-plan area was already set for two, with several candles placed in its centre waiting to be lit, and a bottle of red wine waiting to be opened.

Jonas turned away from the intimacy of that setting to look at Mac instead. Her hair was loose again this evening, and she had changed out of the black jumper, jeans and red body-warmer, into an overlarge thigh-length long-sleeved red shirt over black leggings, with calf-high black boots.

Jonas had spent the remainder of the afternoon telling himself what a bad idea it was for him to come here again this evening. One look at Mac and he didn't give a damn how bad an idea it was, he was just enjoying being in her company again.

'Here.' He handed her the bag of Indian food before thrusting his hands into his jeans pockets in an effort not to reach out, as he so wanted to do, and pull her close to him. Jonas knew that once he had done that he wouldn't want to let her go again. That he would forget everything else but having her in his arms...

Mac turned away from the stark intensity of Jonas's gaze to carry the bag of food over to the breakfast bar and take out the hot cartons before removing the lids with determined concentration, feeling strangely shy in his company now that she was aware of—if choosing not to look too closely at—the feelings she had for him.

'Ben and Jerry did a good job painting over the graffiti,' she told him conversationally as she carried the warmed plates and cartons of food over to the table on a tray.

Jonas shrugged. 'It's too dark for me to tell.'

Mac nodded. 'They were very efficient.' Her gaze didn't quite meet his as she straightened and turned, at the same time completely aware of how vibrantly attractive he looked in a blue cashmere sweater, the same colour as his eyes, and faded jeans of a lighter blue.

'Mac…?'

She raised her eyes to look at him before as quickly looking away again as she felt that familiar thrill of awareness down the length of her spine. 'We should sit down and eat before the food gets cold.'

Jonas frowned at the awkwardness he could feel growing between them. 'Mac, are you even going to look at me?'

She leant back against the table as she turned and raised startled lids, her eyes huge grey orbs in the paleness of her face, her expression pained. 'What are we doing, Jonas?' she groaned huskily.

He gave a rueful shrug. 'Eating dinner together, I thought.'

She shook her head. 'After agreeing only this afternoon that it was a *bad* idea!'

'No, *you* said it was a bad idea. I don't think you asked for my opinion,' Jonas recalled dryly. Although, if asked at the time, he would have said it was a bad idea, too! 'As you said, the food is getting cold, so I suggest that for now we just sit down and eat and think about this again later?' He moved to pointedly pull back one of the chairs for her to sit down.

Mac regarded him quizzically as she sat. 'You really do like having your own way, don't you?'

'Almost as much as you enjoy doing the exact opposite of what you know I want,' Jonas acknowledged with a quick smile as he sat down opposite her before picking up the bottle of wine and deftly opening it.

Mac chuckled softly. 'Interesting.'

'Irritating for the main part, actually,' Jonas admitted as he poured the wine into their glasses. He raised his own glass and made a toast. 'To—hopefully—our first indigestion-free meal together!'

Mac raised her glass and touched it gently against the side of Jonas's. 'To an indigestion-free meal!' she echoed huskily, not too sure about the 'first' part of the toast. It implied there might be other meals to come, and, as Mac knew only too well, she and Jonas always ended up arguing if they spent any length of time together.

Well...almost always. The times when they didn't argue were even more disturbing...

'You really do like Christmas, don't you?'

Mac looked up from helping herself to some of the food in the cartons to see Jonas was looking at her brightly decked Christmas tree. 'I would have said, doesn't everyone?' she replied. 'But I already know that you don't.'

'I wouldn't go that far,' Jonas said.

'No?' Mac eyed him interestedly.

He shrugged. 'I don't dislike Christmas, Mac, it's just a time I remember when my parents were forced to spend a couple of days in each other's company, with the result they usually ended up having one almighty slanging match before the holiday was over. As my grandmother died on Christmas Eve, Joseph wasn't particularly into celebrating it, either.'

'What about your cousin Amy and her family?'

'Amy always goes away with her partner for Christmas, and I'm not close to my uncle and aunt. What can I say?' he drawled at Mac's dismayed expression. 'We're a dysfunctional family.'

It sounded awful to Mac when she thought of her own happy childhood, and the wonderful memories she had of family Christmases, both in the distant past and more recently. 'Why did you call your grandfather Joseph?'

Jonas gave a humourless smile. 'Calling out "Granddad" on a building site didn't go down too well with him, so it became a habit to call him by his first name.'

Looking at Jonas now, so suave, so obviously wealthy from the car he drove and the penthouse apartment he lived in, it was difficult to envision him as a rough and tough teenager working on a building site.

Yet there were those calluses Mac had noticed on his palms three days ago. And there was a ripcord strength about Jonas that didn't look as if it came solely from working out in a gym. Wealthy or not, underneath all that suave sophistication, she realised he was still capable of being every bit as rough and tough as he had been as a teenager.

'What?' Jonas paused in eating his food to look across at her questioningly.

Mac shrugged. 'I was just thinking that maybe you should think about starting your own Christmas traditions.'

From the way Mac had been looking at him so search-ingly Jonas was pretty sure that hadn't been what she had been thinking at all. Although quite what she had been thinking, he had no idea.

She was still something of an enigma to him, he recognised ruefully. There was no sophisticated game-playing with Mac. No artifice. As she had so emphati-cally told him, what you saw was what you got. And what Jonas saw he wanted very badly indeed...

He sighed. 'It's never seemed worth the bother when I only have myself to think about.'

Mac looked at him assessingly. 'I'm taking a bet that you usually go away for Christmas. Somewhere hot,' she qualified. 'Golden sandy beaches where you can sunbathe, and there are waiters to bring you tall drinks with exotic fruit and umbrellas in them. Somewhere you can forget it even is Christmas,' she teased.

'You would win your bet,' Jonas acknowledged with a smile.

She shook her head. 'I can't imagine ever going away for Christmas.'

Neither could Jonas when he could clearly see the distaste on Mac's face. 'What do you and your family do over Christmas?' he asked.

Those beautiful smoky grey eyes glowed. 'Nowadays we all converge on my parents' house in a little village called Tulnerton in Devon. My mother's parents, sev-eral aged aunts. All the presents are placed under the tree, and Christmas Eve we all have a family meal and then attend Midnight Mass at the local church together. When we get back Mum and I usually put the turkey in the oven so that it cooks slowly overnight and the house is full of the smells of it cooking in the morning when we sit down to open our presents. When I was younger, that sometimes happened as early as five o'clock in the morning,' she recalled wistfully. 'Nowadays it's usually about nine o'clock, after we've checked on the turkey and everyone has a cup of tea.'

Jonas's mouth twisted. 'The perfect Christmas indeed.'

Mac eyed him ruefully. 'To me it is, yes.'

Jonas reached out and placed his hand over hers as it rested on the tabletop. 'I wasn't mocking you, Mac,' he said gruffly.

'No?'

Strangely enough, no... It was all too easy for Jonas to envisage the Christmas Mac described so warmly. The sort of Christmas that many families strived for and never actually experienced. The sort of Christmas Jonas had never had. And never would have.

'There are no arguments?' he prompted.

Her eyes glowed with laughter. 'Usually only over who's going to pull the wishbone after we've eaten our Christmas lunch!'

His fingers curled about hers. 'It sounds wonderful.'

Mac was very aware of the air of intimacy that now surrounded the two of them. But it was a different type of intimacy from a physical one. This intimacy was warm and enveloping. Dangerous...

She removed her hand purposefully from beneath Jonas's to pick up her fork. 'I'm sure there must have been arguments; you can't put eight or ten disparate people in a house together for four or five days without there being the odd disagreement. I've obviously just chosen to forget them.' She grimaced.

Jonas looked across at her with enigmatic blue eyes.

'You don't have to make excuses for your own happy childhood, Mac.'

'I wasn't—'

'Weren't you?' he rasped.

Yes, she supposed she had been. Because Jonas's childhood had borne absolutely no resemblance to her own. Because, although he wouldn't thank her for it in the slightest, her heart ached for him. 'If you haven't made other plans yet, perhaps you would like to—' Mac broke off abruptly, her cheeks warming as she realised how utterly ridiculous she was being.

Jonas eyed her warily. 'Please tell me you weren't about to invite me to spend Christmas with you and your family in Devon.'

That was exactly what Mac had been about to do! Impulsively. Stupidly! Of course Jonas didn't want to spend Christmas with her, let alone the rest of her family; with half a dozen strangers there, as well as Mac herself, he would necessarily have to be polite to everyone for the duration of his stay.

Her cheeks were now positively burning with embarrassment. 'I think I feel that indigestion coming on!'

Jonas studied Mac through narrowed lids, knowing by her evasiveness that she *had* been about to invite him to spend Christmas with her and her family. Why? Because she actually wanted to spend Christmas with him? Or because she felt sorry for him and just couldn't bear the thought of anyone—even him—spending Christmas alone?

His mouth thinned. 'I don't recall ever saying that I'm *alone* when I spend my Christmases sunbathing on those golden sandy beaches.'

'No, you didn't, did you?' The colour had left Mac's cheeks as quickly as it had warmed them, her eyes a huge and haunted grey as she gave a moue of self-disgust. 'How naïve of me.'

Jonas knew that he had deliberately hit out at her because pity was the last thing he wanted from her. From anyone. Damn it, he was successful and rich and could afford to do anything he wanted to do. He had never met refusal from any woman he'd shown an interest in taking to his bed. All the things he had decided he wanted out of life years ago when he left university so determined to succeed he had achieved.

Then why did just being with Mac like this, talking with her, make him just as aware of all the things he *didn't* have in his life?

Things like having someone to come home to every night. The same someone. To share things with. To laugh with. To make love with.

'Don't knock it until you've tried it,' Jonas drawled. 'In fact, why don't you consider giving the traditional family Christmas a miss this year and come away with me instead?' he asked as he looked at her over the top of his wine glass before lifting it and taking a deep swallow of the ruby-red liquid.

Mac stared at Jonas, absolutely incredulous that he appeared to be asking her to go away with him for Christmas.

CHAPTER TEN

WAS Jonas serious about his invitation? Or was he just playing with her, already knowing from her earlier remarks exactly what her answer would be?

One look at the unmistakable mockery on his ruggedly handsome face and Mac knew that was exactly what he was doing.

She stood up. 'It would serve you right if I said yes!' she snapped as she picked up her glass of wine and moved across the room to stand beside the Christmas tree.

'Try me,' Jonas invited as he relaxed back in his chair to look across at her thoughtfully. 'I assure you, if you said yes then I would book two first-class seats on a flight that would allow us to arrive in Barbados on Christmas Eve,' he promised huskily.

Mac looked at him scornfully. 'That's so easy to say when you knew before you even asked that I would refuse.'

'Did I?' He stood up to slowly cross the room, his piercing blue gaze easily holding hers captive as he came to a halt only inches away from her.

Mac stared up at him, her breathing somehow feeling constricted. She moistened her lips with the tip of her tongue. 'I had already told you that I couldn't imagine spending Christmas anywhere but at home with my parents.'

Jonas's dark gaze was fixed on those moist and slightly parted lips. 'I'm curious to know what your answer would have been if that family Christmas was taken out of the equation?'

Mac gave a firm shake of her head. 'I hate even the idea of spending Christmas on a beach.'

Jonas had no idea why he was even pursuing this conversation. Except perhaps that he wanted to know if Mac's invitation for him to spend Christmas with her family had been out of the pity he suspected it was, or something else… 'What if I were to suggest we went to a ski resort instead of a beach?'

She smiled slightly. 'I can't ski.'

'I don't recall saying anything about the two of us actually going skiing. I seriously doubt I would have any desire to leave our bedroom once we got there,' Jonas admitted wickedly.

Once again her cheeks coloured with that becoming blush. 'Wouldn't that rather defeat the object?'

He gave a shrug. 'Surely that would depend on what the objective was?'

Mac looked up at him and frowned. 'I believe we had this conversation three days ago, Jonas. At which time, I believe you made it *more* than clear that you're not at all interested in becoming my first lover.'

He hadn't been. He still wasn't. Except he had realised these last three days that he didn't like the thought of some other man being Mac's first lover either! 'Maybe I've changed my mind,' he replied guardedly.

'And maybe you just enjoying playing games with me,' Mac said knowingly.

'Mac, I haven't even begun to play games with you

yet!' he teased. Although whether that teasing was directed at her or himself, Jonas wasn't sure...

He wanted to make love with this woman. He actually wanted it so badly he could taste it. Taste *her*.

Dear God, there were so many ways he could make love to this woman without actually taking her virginity. So many ways he could give her incredible pleasure. And she could give him that same pleasure in return.

But would it be enough to sate the ever-rising hunger inside him? Would touching Mac, caressing her, making love to her but never actually taking her, being inside her, ever be enough for him? Did he really have that much self-control?

Where she was concerned? Somehow Jonas doubted it! The only reason they hadn't already become lovers when she had been at his apartment was because of the realisation of the seemingly insurmountable barrier of her virginity.

Jonas moved away abruptly. 'You're right, this conversation is pointless. Christmas is still two weeks away—'

'And we may not even be talking to each other again by then!' Mac put in with black humour.

'Probably not,' he admitted. 'But even if we are, we still both know that you will be spending Christmas in Devon with your family and I will be sitting on a beach somewhere improving my tan.'

Mac didn't think that Jonas's tan needed improving; his skin was already a deep gold. And from the calluses on his hands and those defined muscles in his shoulders and chest, she didn't think that tan had been acquired sitting on a beach anywhere!

In fact, if she had arrived home a little later than she had this morning, then she was pretty sure that she would have found Jonas up that metal tower outside her home beside Ben and Jerry as he helped to paint over the graffiti. Jonas might now be rich and powerful, the owner of his own company for some years rather than an employee, but his rugged appearance and weather-hewn features were testament to the fact that he still enjoyed getting his hands dirty occasionally.

'I was totally sincere in my invitation for you to spend Christmas with my family, Jonas,' she said huskily.

His eyes were a hard and mocking blue. 'And what do you think your family would have made of you bringing a man home for the holidays?'

Mac's cheeks warmed as she easily imagined her father's teasing, and the whispered speculation of her aged aunts, if Jonas had accepted her invitation and accompanied her to Devon. 'Oh.' She grimaced. 'I hadn't really thought of that.'

'Exactly,' Jonas said, drinking the last of his wine before placing the empty glass on the table. 'It's probably time I was going.'

Mac blinked. 'It's still early.'

As far as Jonas was concerned, it was seriously bordering on being too late!

She looked so damned beautiful, so desirable with the coloured lights on the tree reflected in the glossy curtain of her long black hair, her eyes a deep and misty grey, her skin like a warm peach, and her lips—dear heaven, those full and pouting lips!

Jonas wanted to take those lips with his own, devour them, to kiss her and explore the hot temptation of her mouth until she felt the same need he did. If he didn't leave here soon, in the next few minutes, he wasn't going to be able to withstand that temptation at all.

'You didn't get to see my studio earlier; would you like to see it now?'

Jonas was jolted out of that rising fiery haze of desire to focus on Mac. 'Sorry…?'

She shrugged narrow shoulders. 'Obviously the studio is pretty empty at the moment with most of my recent work being at the exhibition, but you're welcome to take a look. If you would like to,' she added almost shyly.

Did he want to do that? He had evaded taking up the invitation earlier because he didn't want to find himself being drawn into Mac's world any more than he already was. To see where she had created the amazing paintings like the ones he had seen at the Lyndwood Gallery the previous week, and to feel himself being pulled even deeper into the intimacy of Mac's life.

He still wanted to avoid doing that, didn't he?

'I would like to,' Jonas instead heard himself accept gruffly.

Mac smiled. 'It's just up the spiral staircase.' She placed her glass down next to Jonas's on the table before turning to lead the way.

Jonas reached out and grasped her arm to look down searchingly into her face, sure by the way she avoided meeting his gaze, that she was already regretting having made the invitation. 'Don't take me up there if you would rather not, Mac…'

'I—no, it's fine,' she reassured him, not really sure that it *was* fine, but unwilling for Jonas to leave just yet.

Because she could sense the air of finality about him now and she had the feeling that once he left this time he would ensure that it really was the last time she saw him.

Yet wasn't that what she wanted? Didn't she want

Jonas out of her life? To never have to see and deal with this disturbing man ever again?

'It will only take a few minutes,' she told him briskly as she pulled out of his grasp and walked over and switched on the light overhead. She'd rather take him up the spiral staircase to her studio than answer any of her own soul-searching questions.

But she was completely aware of Jonas, every step of the way, as he followed behind her up that metal staircase…

Whatever he had been expecting Mac's studio to look like, after the warmth and colour of the living area below, it certainly wasn't the starkness of the pale cream colour-wash on the three bare brick walls. Or the fourth wall that faced towards the river completely glass, the ceiling also made up of glass panels, and revealing the clear star-lit sky overhead. The only furniture in the room was an old and faded chaise against one wall and a daybed beside another.

Mac's easel was set up near the huge glass window, and she strolled across the room to lightly lay a cover over the painting she was currently working on. 'I never allow people to see my work before it's completed,' she explained ruefully at Jonas's questioning look.

The surroundings weren't quite 'starving in a garret', but the studio was much more basic than Jonas had been expecting after the vividness of colours on the floor below. 'You prefer not to have any outside distractions when you're working,' he realised softly.

Mac turned to him with wide eyes. 'No…'

She hadn't expected him to have that insight, Jonas realised, wondering if anyone else had ever really understood how and why she worked in the surroundings she did. Surroundings that were unique in the way Mac had converted this warehouse to her own individual needs.

Another reason she refused to sell the warehouse to Buchanan Construction. The main reason probably; most of Mac's emotional links to her grandfather would be inside her rather than consisting of bricks and mortar.

This last realisation put Jonas in an untenable position.

Had she done that deliberately?

His mouth thinned as he turned to look at Mac. 'You brought me up here for a purpose.'

Mac briefly thought of denying it, and then thought better of it as she recognised the steely glitter in Jonas's eyes. 'I'm not sure I could work anywhere else,' she answered truthfully.

'Have you ever tried?' he gritted.

'No. But—' She moved her shoulders in an uncomfortable shrug. 'I just thought it might help if you understood I'm not just being bloody-minded by refusing to sell my home and my studio to you.'

'You thought by showing me this that I would back off,' Jonas guessed. 'I don't enjoy being manipulated, Mac,' he said coolly.

She frowned. 'I wasn't—'

'Yes, you were, damn you!' he burst out, suddenly explosive in his anger, taking the two long strides that brought him to within touching distance of her. 'This is just an artist's studio, Mac. It could be replicated just about anywhere.'

She shook her head. 'You're wrong. I've lived and worked here for the past five years—'

'And once this place has been knocked down you'll live and work somewhere else for a lot longer than that!' he said grimly.

'I told you, that isn't going to happen—' Her protest was cut short as Jonas reached out to pull her into his arms before lowering his head and grinding his mouth fiercely down onto hers.

It was a kiss of punishment rather than gentleness, anger rather than passion, Jonas's arms like steel bands about her waist as he held her tightly against him, pressing her to his muscled body, making Mac completely aware of the pulsing hardness of his thighs.

She stood on tiptoe as her hands moved up his chest to his shoulders, and then into the dark thickness of the hair at his nape, her mouth slanting, lips parting beneath his as she returned the heat of that kiss.

Jonas was aware of his shift in mood as the angry need to punish her faded and passion and desire took over, groaning low in his throat as he began to sip and taste the softness of Mac's lips, his tongue stroking those lips as he tested their sweetness before moving deeper into the hot and welcoming warmth of Mac's mouth.

He could feel her delicacy beneath the restless caress of his hands down the length of her spine before he cupped her bottom to pull her up and into him, the soft and welcoming well between her thighs both an agony and an ecstasy as his arousal fitted perfectly against her.

He dragged his mouth from hers to breathe deeply against her creamy cheek. 'Wrap your legs around me,' he encouraged fiercely.

'I don't—'

'I promise I'll lift and support you, Mac,' he looked up to encourage hotly. 'I just need you to wrap your legs around me,' he exhorted her gruffly before burying his lips against the side of her neck.

Jonas's tongue was a fiery torment against Mac's

skin, a rasping, arousing torment that made her feel weak and wanting even as she did as he asked. As promised, Jonas's hands beneath her bottom easily lifted and supported her as she raised up to curve her legs about him and instantly felt the press of his arousal against the centre of her parted thighs.

Her thin leggings and brief panties were no barrier to that firm and pulsating flesh as it pressed against her. Mac felt herself swell there, becoming damp, wet, so hot and aching as Jonas's mouth claimed hers once again.

She was barely aware of him carrying her across the room to press her against the wall, Mac only realising he had done so as the coldness of the brick against her back became a sharp counterpoint to the heated arousal of her breasts and thighs.

His arousal was more penetrating now, pressing into that welcoming well as Jonas moved against her rhythmically, each thrust of his body matched by the penetration of his tongue into the heated inferno of her mouth, so that Mac felt him everywhere.

Jonas wrenched his mouth from hers, breathing hard as he looked down at her with fiercely dark eyes. 'I'm going to pleasure you, Mac,' he promised gruffly as he carried her over to lay her down on the chaise. 'I'm going to make love to you until you beg me to stop,' he vowed as he knelt on the floor beside the chaise.

He pushed her shirt out of the way and took off her boots, then peeled away her leggings and panties before moving up to kneel between her parted thighs. 'You're so beautiful here, Mac,' he murmured throatily as he looked down at her hungrily. He reached out to touch her naked thighs, fingers gentle as he parted her ebony curls.

Mac moaned as she felt Jonas's fingers move against

her in a light caress, heat coursing through her body as that pressure increased, that moan turning to a breathless keening as she felt a burning, aching pressure building inside her, demanding, wanting, needing—

'Jonas!' she cried out at the first intimate touch of his mouth against her, the moistness of his tongue a soft caress against her tender and aching skin.

Her hands moved restlessly, fingers threading into Jonas's hair with the intention of stopping that unbearable torment, but instead finding her fingers tightening her hold as she pressed him closer still, arching into him as she felt the probe of his fingers against her entrance, so close, so very close, and yet circling just out of reach.

'Yes, Jonas!' Mac groaned her torment as she pressed urgently against those tormenting fingers. 'Please…!'

God, how Jonas needed this, wanted this; the taste of Mac in his mouth and the feel of how hot and ready she was beneath his caressing hands.

He entered her slowly as he continued to use his tongue to flicker against her. His fingers began to thrust, slowly, gently to the rhythm of Mac's low encouraging groans as she moved urgently until her muscles tightened and she climaxed in long and beautiful spasms that caused her to cry out in mindless pleasure.

Mac had never felt anything like this in her life before, the pleasure so incredible it bordered on pain. Wave after wave of heat coursing, singing through her body as Jonas continued the relentless pressure of his lips and tongue until he had extracted every last vestige of her climax.

It seemed minutes, hours later, that Mac finally collapsed weakly back onto the chaise, her breath a choking sob, her body so alive to his every touch, so tinglingly aware, that she almost couldn't bear it.

Almost...

Jonas began to kiss his way up the flatness of her belly, unbuttoning her shirt to expose her naked breasts to the ministrations of the heat of his mouth, first one breast and then the other, the rasp of his jeans against her inner thighs as he lay half across her an added torment to her roused and sensitive body.

His hair looked so dark against the whiteness of her skin as Mac looked down at him, his lips fastened about one nipple as his fingers caressed its twin.

Incredibly Mac felt her pleasure rising again. More intense this time, deeper. Every touch, every caress causing her body to quiver in awareness. 'I want to touch you, too, Jonas.' She moved until she was sitting up slightly. 'I need to touch you,' she added achingly as he looked up at her, his eyes dark and heavy with arousal.

Jonas studied her searchingly; her eyes were fever bright, her cheeks flushed, her lips... He had never seen anything as sensual as Mac's pouting, full lips, could feel himself hardening to steel as he easily imagined those lips about him and her hair falling silkily across his hips and thighs as she pleasured him.

The image was so clear, so urgent, that Jonas offered no resistance as she sat up fully to push him down onto the chaise beneath her before unbuttoning and unzipping his jeans to slide them and his boxers far enough down his thighs to fully expose his hard and jutting erection. He groaned low in his throat as he saw the way Mac looked at him so hungrily before she reached out tentatively and wrapped her fingers about him.

She loved caressing him and learning what gave

Jonas the most pleasure as her hand began to move up and down.

Jonas's hands clenched at his sides as that pleasure held him as tightly in its grip as Mac did. His focus became fixed on the expression on her face as she continued to touch him. The fascination. The pleasure. Then the eroticism of seeing the moist tip of her tongue moving over her lips before she slowly lowered her head towards him, before she finally took him into her mouth.

Jonas's back arched as he thrust up into that heat, the past week or so of wanting this woman, making love to her so far but never taking her, making it impossible for him to temper his own response. That response spiralled out of control as she took him deeper into her mouth before slowly drawing back. Then repeating it all over again. Setting a rhythm, a tormenting, heated rhythm that Jonas had no will or desire to resist.

Jonas became lost in that bombardment of sensations, breathing hard, and then not breathing at all when he felt his exquisite release in mindless, beautiful pleasure.

CHAPTER ELEVEN

MAC could feel and hear Jonas breathing raggedly beside her as her head lay against his chest. Jonas's arms were wrapped tightly about her as the two of them lay side by side on the chaise. Her thoughts were racing as she wondered what happened now. Now that Jonas knew her—and her body—more intimately than anyone else ever had. Now that she knew Jonas's body more intimately than she had any other man's...

That she had been able to give him the same pleasure he had given her filled her with an immense feeling of satisfaction. But it was a satisfaction tempered by uncertainty. By the knowledge that her emotions, while she didn't want to look at them too deeply here and now, were most definitely involved. And she had no idea whether or not she would ever see Jonas again after tonight...

Neither of them had spoken as they'd adjusted their clothing into some semblance of order before they lay down together on the chaise. Mac knew her own silence was because she felt a somewhat gauche awkwardness following the intensity of their lovemaking. But she had absolutely no idea what Jonas was thinking or feeling as he lay so silently beside her.

'This is usually the awkward part.' Jonas's chest rumbled beneath Mac's ear as he finally spoke.

Mac could feel the rapid beat of her own heart. The plummeting beat of her heart. Surely this could only be awkward if Jonas didn't intend seeing her again?

'Extracting oneself without embarrassment, you mean?' she guessed huskily.

'Something like that.'

He hadn't intended things to go as far between them as they had. He had wanted to make love to Mac, to give her pleasure. But he hadn't expected to receive that same pleasure back, or for that pleasure to be given so completely. So beautifully. So erotically he had been unable to stop himself from climaxing.

There had been many women in Jonas's life the last fifteen years. Or, rather, in his bed; he didn't allow any woman to actually be a part of his life.

In the past those relationships had always been based on Jonas's need for physical release, and the woman's need for a bed partner who was wealthy enough to treat them out of bed in the way they enjoyed, to be wined and dined and bought the odd piece of expensive jewellery. As far as Jonas was concerned, it had been a fair exchange of needs. Almost as cut and dried as a business proposition, in fact. Something he could definitely relate to.

He didn't understand this relationship with Mac at all...

In fact, Jonas shied away from even calling it that.

That they had met at all had been purely accidental, a business necessity. Their meetings since had, for the main part, been just as incidental. Oh, Jonas had known it was her exhibition he was attending, and after their unsatisfactory conversation a few days earlier he had enjoyed seeing her discomfort when he'd arrived at the gallery with Amy.

But the number of times the two of them had met since weren't so easily explained away.

His desire to see her again after tonight was even less so...

It would be insanity on his part to ask to see her again. A complication he didn't need in his life; Mac was nothing at all like any of the women he had known in the past. Jonas doubted he would be able to extricate himself from a relationship with her as easily as he had with those other women.

No, he couldn't see Mac McGuire again.

Not couldn't, *wouldn't*!

He had told Mac more about himself in the time he had known her than he had ever confided in anyone. Even Joel Baxter, who had become a good friend the past twelve years. He had allowed Mac to get below his defences, Jonas realised. To reach him, know him, better than anyone else ever had.

Scx was one thing, but it was definitely time to sever the unwitting friendship that had been developing between them.

Mac looked up just in time to see the grimness of his expression. And to guess the reason for it. Well, she might have been stupid enough to lose her heart to Jonas Buchanan, but that didn't mean she had lost her pride too!

'You needn't look so worried, Jonas,' she assured him dryly as she pulled out of his arms to stand up. Luckily her shirt was thigh length, long enough to hide her nakedness beneath. 'This evening was—different. But I'm in no hurry to repeat the experience.'

Jonas scowled darkly as he sat up and smoothed the

untidy thickness of his hair back from his face. Hair that had felt silky and soft beneath Mac's fingers only minutes ago!

'Are you trying to tell me you didn't *enjoy* it?' he growled incredulously.

Mac raised a cool eyebrow. 'That would be rather silly of me, wouldn't it? No, Jonas,' she added firmly, chin raised. 'I'm not saying that at all. Only that while this evening was—pleasant, sexual gratification is no reason for the two of us to see each other again after tonight.'

It was exactly the same conclusion that Jonas had come to only minutes ago, but hearing her echo that conclusion so emotionlessly irritated the hell out of him. Mac thought the evening had been *pleasant*! Damn it, he had never, ever lost it in the way he had with her tonight. Had never allowed himself to lose control in the way he had earlier when Mac took him into her mouth.

Jonas could still feel that pleasure. The most gut-wrenching, soul-deep pleasure that he had ever known. He knew the memory of it was going to haunt his days and fill his nights for longer than he cared to think about.

He stood up, eyes glittering angrily. 'In other words, you've had your fun, and thanks for the experience?'

She eyed him mildly. 'You seem angry, Jonas. Isn't this what you wanted?'

Yes, damn it, of course it was what he wanted!

Jonas had wanted to be able to extricate himself from this situation with as little unpleasantness between them as possible. Except he had discovered it was something else entirely for Mac to want to do the same thing!

'Whatever,' he snapped coldly. 'I suggest—what the

hell was that?' He scowled darkly as he heard a loud crashing noise coming from outside.

Mac looked totally bewildered. 'I have no idea…'

Jonas strode quickly over to the window that faced over the river, looking out into the darkness. He couldn't actually see anything, or anyone, and his car was still parked in the street below, but he was pretty sure that crashing noise had been the sound of glass breaking.

He turned quickly, his expression grim as he hurried over to the spiral staircase. 'I think your intruder is back!'

Mac had been rooted to the spot, shocked into immobility by the loud sound. But she moved now, hurrying over to stand at the top of the staircase and look down at Jonas as he reached the bottom step. 'You can't go out there alone, Jonas—'

He paused to look up at her. 'Of course I'm going out there,' he said.

'You can't.' Mac shook her head worriedly. 'What if they have a knife? Or—or a gun—'

'You've been watching too much television, Mac,' he said gently.

'There was a stabbing in this area only a couple of weeks ago,' she protested.

'Reportedly rival gangs sorting out the pecking order,' he reassured her.

'Yes, but—'

'Just put some clothes on and call the police, and then wait inside until I come back and give the all-clear,' Jonas told her grimly.

'But—'

'You are *not* to come outside, Mac,' he instructed firmly. 'Do you understand?'

Mac felt her cheeks warm with displeasure, both with

Jonas's high-handed attitude and the reminder that she still didn't have all her clothes on. 'I'm not stupid, Jonas. Neither do I intend just cowering in here while you go outside and face goodness knows what!'

'You'll do as you're damn well told if you don't want me to come back and deal with you once I've dealt with what's going on outside!' he growled.

'You could try,' she seethed.

Jonas's mouth tightened as there was another sound of glass breaking. 'I really don't have time for this right now, Mac. Just do as I ask and don't complicate the situation by forcing me to worry about your safety when I should be concentrating on putting an end to this!' He didn't stay to argue with her any further before disappearing from the bottom of the stairs.

Mac heard the outside door closing seconds later, her heart pounding erratically as she quickly grabbed up her leggings and panties before hurrying down the metal staircase to use her mobile and call the police, her hand shaking so badly she could barely press the right three buttons.

She had to calm down. Had to at least try to be coherent when she gave the necessary information to the police.

Despite those inner warnings Mac knew she sounded slightly hysterical as she talked to the dispatcher who answered.

She hadn't just sounded hysterical, Mac acknowledged after she had ended the call and hurried over to the picture window to look outside. She had sounded frantic.

Because she didn't care who was outside, or what damage they had done to her home this time. All she cared about was Jonas. That he should come back safely.

Mac might have been uncertain about her feelings for Jonas until tonight, but she had absolutely no doubts now that she had fallen totally in love with him...

Jonas knew he was white-faced by the time he wearily accompanied Mac back up the stairs and into the living area of her home almost an hour later.

Who would have guessed it?

Who could have known?

He gave a heavy sigh. 'I told the police I would join them down at the station as soon as possible.' He picked up his jacket and slipped it on, all without looking at Mac.

He couldn't look at her. Couldn't bear to see the accusation that was sure to be in her face.

It had all been his fault, he realised numbly. The initial break-in. The graffiti. The windows broken this evening on Mac's Jeep parked downstairs in the garage. All of it was Jonas's fault.

He hadn't known. Hadn't realised. Despite Mac's teasing remark earlier in the week, he had still never guessed that Yvonne had feelings for him; the sort of feelings that had prompted his PA into trying to scare Mac into selling the warehouse to Jonas.

'Drink some of this first.'

Jonas looked up to see that Mac had refilled his wine glass and now held it out to him. As if wine were going to erase the horror of finding Yvonne downstairs systematically breaking the windows on Mac's car. Or numb his disbelief at the conversation that had followed. The hysterical conviction Yvonne had that she was helping him. That she loved him. Was sure the two of them were meant to be together.

All of it made worse by the fact that Mac had disobeyed his instruction by then and come downstairs to join him, hearing every word Yvonne said. Along with the police who had arrived only minutes earlier.

Nothing could ever erase the horror of any of that from Jonas's mind!

He grimaced. 'I don't think it's a good idea for me to arrive at a police station smelling of alcohol.'

Probably not, Mac acknowledged as she put the wine glass down on the table.

What an evening! She and Jonas had made love. Mac had realised—and still shied away from looking at it too deeply—that she was in love with Jonas. And now this.

By the time she had dressed and hurried downstairs to the garage, Yvonne Richards had been in full spate, professing her love for Jonas, explaining that she had only terrorised Mac because she wanted to help him. That she had only done those things in an effort to convince Mac into selling the warehouse to Buchanan Construction.

This whole evening had been surreal from start to finish. And it wasn't over yet!

'Would it help if I told the police I have no intention of pressing charges?' Mac asked softly; Yvonne Richards seemed more in need of psychiatric help than prosecution!

Jonas's expression was bleak. 'I have no idea.' He gave a slightly dazed shake of his head as he sat down suddenly. 'I— Do you think Yvonne has done anything like this before? Tried to "help me" like this before?' He frowned darkly as the possibility occurred to him.

Mac shrugged. 'Let's not even go there, Jonas. It's the here and now that we have to deal with,' she added cajolingly. 'Perhaps I should come to the police station with you—'

'No!' Jonas refused harshly as he stood up. He felt humiliated enough for one evening, without Mac having to hear—yet again—how Yvonne had only done the things she had because she was in love with him.

How or why that had happened, Jonas had no idea. Yvonne had worked for him as his PA for almost two years now. She had proved to be particularly good at her job, and as far as Jonas was concerned the two of them had an excellent working relationship. Obviously there had been business trips they had taken together, as well as long hours spent alone together, but Jonas was sure there had never been the slightest suggestion on his part that the two of them had any sort of personal relationship.

He looked across at Mac. 'I've never given Yvonne the slightest encouragement to feel the way she says she feels about me.' He rubbed the back of his neck. 'To my knowledge I've never so much as touched her or spoken to her in a way that could possibly be misconstrued as sexual interest.'

Mac knew that her gaze didn't quite meet his. 'I'm sure you haven't—'

'Don't patronise me, Mac,' Jonas rasped harshly, eyes narrowing to steely slits. 'I do *not* have relationships with the people who work for or with me. Besides complicating things unnecessarily, it's bad business practice.'

'And why bother when there are so many other women willing to give you what you want?' she came back tartly.

'Was that comment really necessary?' Jonas snarled.

Was it? Probably not. But Mac was feeling less than composed herself after their lovemaking earlier this evening.

She and Jonas had made beautiful and erotic love to each other. At least…it was love on Mac's side. She doubted Jonas's feelings went any further than lust.

It just seemed too much to now learn that she had been terrorised this past week by another woman suffering from that same unrequited love for him!

Mac accepted that it wasn't his fault. Jonas had made it clear from the beginning that he didn't even believe in love, let alone a committed relationship, and so it wasn't his fault if the women he met were stupid enough to fall in love with him.

But that didn't mean Mac couldn't feel a little angry and resentful about it! 'You had better go,' she said distantly.

Jonas knew he had to go. That he should drive to the police station where they had taken Yvonne and try to make some sort of sense out of this ludicrous situation. He would just prefer not to leave things so strained between himself and Mac.

'I'll come back later—'

'I would prefer it if you didn't,' Mac cut in firmly. 'We have nothing else to say to each other, Jonas,' she reasoned as a scowl creased his brow.

'Don't you even want to know what's going to happen to Yvonne?' he asked tonelessly.

She shrugged. 'I'm sure the police will inform me if I need to be involved any further.'

In other words, Jonas realised darkly, Mac considered her 'involvement' with him to be at an end.

Like hell it was!

He reached out and gripped the tops of her arms. 'I'm coming back later, Mac,' he insisted determinedly. 'If nothing else, you and I need to talk about this evening—'

'There's nothing else to say.' Mac wrenched out of his grasp, her cheeks fiery red. Whether in temper or embarrassment, Jonas wasn't sure. 'I'm grateful for the experience, of course, but I certainly don't want to have a post-mortem about it!'

Temper, Jonas acknowledged. Maybe tinged with a little embarrassment…

He should just cut his losses. Take the opportunity Mac was giving him to extricate himself from this situation with a little grace allowed to remain on both sides.

Yet looking at her he couldn't help but remember how he had kissed her. Touched her. Pleasured her. Just as she had kissed and touched and pleasured him.

'I'm coming back later,' he repeated firmly.

'I'm going to bed as soon as I've locked up behind you and cleared away,' she argued just as stubbornly.

Jonas's mouth twisted. 'Then you'll just have to get out of bed and unlock the door and let me in again, won't you?'

Her mouth compressed. 'Don't you understand that I don't want you here, Jonas?'

'I would have to be pretty stupid not to realise that when you've said it three times in as many minutes,' he commented.

Mac had never felt so—so frustrated, so irritated with anyone in her life before. 'Isn't finding out one woman is in love with you enough for one evening?' she shot back.

'Low blow, Mac,' Jonas muttered between clenched teeth, his face paling one more.

It was a low blow. Not only that, it was spiteful when Jonas's shock earlier at learning of his PA's feelings for him had been self-evident. 'Sorry,' she murmured uncomfortably. 'I'm just not sure you should come back here later.'

'Why not?'

Mac moved away restlessly. 'Frankly, I find this whole situation embarrassing,' she admitted. 'I— We— Earlier—' She shook her head. 'Maybe you're used to these situations, Jonas, but I'm not.' And she never would be. Not if the cringing awkwardness she now felt with Jonas was any indication of how traumatic it was to be in the company of a man you had been intimate with. A man you were in love with but who didn't, and never would, love you back...

It was no good telling herself how stupid it was to have allowed her emotions to become involved with a man like Jonas. No good at all when she knew herself to be deeply, irrevocably, in love with him. In the circumstances, her only option had to be never to see him again!

'I really can't take any more tonight, Jonas,' she told him with quiet conviction. 'I just want to go to bed, fall asleep, and hope that when I wake up in the morning I'll find that this whole evening has been just a nightmare.'

Jonas had never heard any woman describe making love with him as a nightmare before, but there had been so many firsts for him with Mac already, why not add that one to the list?

His mouth firmed. 'I'm not quite sure what you're referring to by "these situations",' he said. 'However,

I do accept—for now—that you feel you want some time alone.' He ran a hand impatiently through the dark thickness of his hair. 'If it's any consolation, this evening didn't turn out the way I expected it to, either.'

Mac gave a humourless smile. 'Nothing ever seems to turn out as "expected" between the two of us.' The fact that she had met the owner of Buchanan Construction at all, let alone made love with him, certainly shouldn't have happened.

'No,' Jonas acknowledged heavily as he studied her for several long minutes before turning sharply and walking over to the door. 'I'll ring you tomorrow.'

Jonas could ring all he wanted; Mac had already decided she wasn't going to be here.

No doubt her parents were going to think it a little odd when she turned up in Devon again so soon after her last visit, but what choice did she have? She couldn't stay in London after tonight. Well…she could. If she wanted to have another embarrassing conversation with Jonas like this last one!

'Fine.'

Jonas's eyes narrowed suspiciously on her suddenly expressionless face. 'What aren't you telling me, Mac?'

She gave a brittle laugh. 'Nothing you want to hear, I assure you!'

Jonas continued to look across at her in utter frustration. Would he still be leaving like this if they hadn't heard the sound of glass breaking downstairs, if he hadn't discovered that it was one of his own employees causing the damage to Mac's property, scaring the hell out of her in the process, and if he didn't now have to go to the local police station and sort the mess out? If none of that had happened, would he now be joining Mac in her bed, or would he have left anyway?

It had certainly been his intention to leave before any of those things happened. For him to get as far away from her disturbing presence as possible. Now the only thing he wanted to do was crawl into bed with her and make love to her all over again. Which, in itself, was reason enough for him to get the hell out of here!

'Make sure you bolt and lock the door behind me,' he advised gruffly.

Mac waited only long enough for Jonas to close the door behind him before quickly crossing the room and doing exactly that, to then turn and lean weakly back against it as her legs threatened to buckle beneath her.

She *had* fallen in love with Jonas Buchanan.

A man who would never love her because he had no time for the emotion.

What was she going to do?

CHAPTER TWELVE

As IT turned out, MAC wasn't able to leave London the following morning as planned, after all.

The telephone rang for the first time just after eight o'clock. Fearing, as promised, that it might be Jonas, Mac reluctantly answered the call, immensely relieved when it turned out to be the police asking if she would come down to the police station this morning so that they might talk to her.

Mac was only too happy to agree—the thought of not being at the warehouse to take Jonas's call, or at home if he actually came to the warehouse in person, was definitely an appealing one.

When she received a second telephone call a few minutes later, from Jeremy this time, asking her if she could call round to the gallery in the afternoon and meet a gallery owner from America who was interested in showing some of her work over there, she was only too happy to have an excuse not to be at the warehouse in the afternoon too.

Besides, the request from the police was one that Mac couldn't avoid or simply ignore, and the one from Jeremy was one she didn't want to avoid or ignore. The possibility of taking her work to America, too, would be a dream come true for her.

Consequently, Mac was forced to remain in London even though it was the last place she wanted to be. Forced to remain, perhaps, but at the same time given two legitimate reasons to avoid speaking to or seeing Jonas while she was here.

At least, until she returned to the warehouse at six o'clock that evening and once again found him sitting waiting for her at the bottom of the metal staircase leading up to her home!

Jonas stood up slowly as Mac came to a brief halt before she resumed walking cautiously towards him, her crash helmet tucked under her arm and her hair shaken loose about her leather-clad shoulders. 'You're a difficult woman to track down,' he commented ruefully.

She shrugged those narrow shoulders as she came to a halt in front of him. 'Is this something important, Jonas, or can it wait until another time? I'm rather busy this evening.'

Jonas's mouth thinned at her dismissive tone. He had spent hours at the police station the previous night, talking, explaining, in the hope of avoiding having the situation go any further than it already had. But it had taken until lunchtime today for the police to telephone and inform him they were prepared not to proceed any further with the case as long as Yvonne sought professional help for her behaviour. At the same time making it clear to him that Mac's refusal to press charges concerning the damage to her property had helped them to make that decision.

Trying to speak to Mac and thank her for her intervention had proved more difficult. She hadn't answered any of Jonas's telephone calls. She hadn't been at home when he'd called round earlier this afternoon. When he'd called at the warehouse a second time about an hour ago, and found she still wasn't at home, Jonas had just decided to sit and wait for her.

'Busy doing what?' he grated harshly.

Her eyes narrowed. 'I don't believe that is any of your business, do you?'

The fact that Mac now made no effort to walk up the steps and go into the warehouse indicated she had no intention of inviting him inside. 'It's too cold to stand out here talking.' The cold vapour on his breath gave truth to that statement.

Her chin rose stubbornly. 'I didn't invite you here, Jonas.'

He reached out and took a light hold of her arm. 'Perhaps not, but now that I *am* here you could be polite and invite me inside.'

Mac eyed him impatiently. 'Why change things now?'

Jonas gave her a humourless smile. 'Meaning we've never particularly bothered being polite to each other before?'

'Exactly!' she said. 'I really do need to shower and change, Jonas.'

'You're going out this evening?'

'Not that it's any of your business, but yes, I'm going out,' she snapped.

Jonas felt his hands clench in the pockets of his long woollen overcoat. 'With whom?'

'That's none of your business, either!' Grey eyes glittered with temper.

His jaw tightened warningly. 'I believe what we did last night made it my business.'

Mac tensed indignantly. 'Like hell it did!' She glared up at Jonas, so angry she could have hit him. 'Last night was a mistake from start to finish. The finish obviously being the revelation that it was your own PA who was vandalising my home and property!'

Jonas scowled darkly. 'You're holding *me* responsible for that?'

'Who else?' Mac came back heatedly, knowing she wasn't being completely fair in that accusation, but feeling too unnerved by finding him here waiting for her to even try to rationalise or calm the situation down. 'There's bound to be some sort of reaction when you play games with people's emotions—'

'I've already told you I've never so much as said a word out of place to Yvonne!' A nerve pulsed in his jaw. 'As far as I'm concerned, she has only ever been my PA, never my mistress, and—'

'Jonas, I don't care what your relationship was with Yvonne Richards.' Mac smiled insincerely. 'I'm just relieved to have the whole sorry mess over and done with.'

His nostrils flared. 'You're including our own relationship in that statement?'

'We don't *have* a relationship, Jonas,' she said flatly.

'Last night—'

'We had sex,' Mac finished coolly. 'Interesting experience, but, as I told you at the time, one I'm in no particular hurry to repeat!'

Jonas eyed her frustratedly. He had sought her out today with the sole intention of thanking her for her help in regards to the situation with Yvonne, and then leaving without making any further arrangements to ever see or be with her again. That she was making it more than obvious she was just as anxious to be rid of him definitely rankled.

Which was pretty stupid of him! 'I just wanted to thank you for your help with Yvonne,' he explained.

'You could have done that over the telephone.'

'I wanted to thank you personally.' His eyes glittered. 'Besides, you weren't answering your phone.'

'I've been out all day.'

'Obviously.' Jonas looked at her broodingly as she made no answer, knowing he should leave, and that Mac herself was giving him the perfect opportunity to do exactly that. Except… 'So, are you going out anywhere interesting this evening?' he prompted lightly.

Her eyes narrowed. 'As I believe I've already told you—I'm not answerable to you for any of my actions, Jonas.'

No, and he had never wanted that from any woman, either. Had never asked for exclusivity from any of the women he had dated in the past. But just the thought of Mac going out with another man was enough to cause a red tide of—of what? What emotion was it that was driving him at this moment? Making it necessary for him to know whom she was seeing this evening?

He straightened. 'I'll leave you to get ready for your evening out then,' he bit out, tersely.

Mac's anger and resentment faded as she looked up at Jonas searchingly and acknowledged the finality she could hear in his tone. 'So this is finally goodbye, then?'

His mouth tightened. 'Only if you want it to be.'

Mac's eyes widened. 'If *I* want it to be?'

He shrugged. 'There's no reason why the two of us shouldn't continue to see each other.'

Not for Jonas, perhaps, but for Mac it would be excruciating to see him, be with him as she longed to be, and know that she loved him while all he felt for her was desire. Knowing that once Jonas had completely sated that desire their relationship would come to an end. As all Jonas's other relationships had ended.

No, Mac's pride wouldn't allow her to take the little that he had to give for as long as he chose to give it. Even if her heart squeezed painfully in her chest at the very idea of never seeing or being with him again...

'Until you got tired of me, you mean?' she guessed shrewdly.

He gave her a half-smile. 'Or you tired of me.'

As if that was ever going to happen!

Mac had waited the whole of her twenty-seven years to meet the man she could love. That she *did* love. It was her misfortune that man happened to be Jonas. A man who didn't even believe in love, let alone in a happy-ever-after forever!

'I don't think so, thank you, Jonas,' she refused dryly.

He scowled darkly. 'Why the hell not?'

Mac shook her head. 'What would be the point? You have your life and I have mine, and the two have absolutely nothing in common.'

Jonas's jaw was clenched. 'Except we want each other!'

Mac smiled sadly. 'Wanting something doesn't mean it's good for you.'

His scowl deepened. 'What the hell does that mean?'

She gave a rueful grimace. 'It means that I know how much I enjoy chocolate, while at the same time accepting that eating too much of it wouldn't be good for me.'

'You're comparing a relationship with me to eating chocolate?'

'It was just an example, Jonas,' she said. 'What I'm really saying is that ultimately the two of us wouldn't be good for each other.'

'We *are* good together,' he contradicted, his voice lowering huskily.

'I said we *wouldn't* be good for each other,' Mac reiterated clearly.

Jonas frowned. 'You can't possibly know that.'

Mac gave a humourless smile. 'Inwardly we both know it, Jonas.'

Yes, inwardly he did know it. Just as he knew Mac was everything that he had always avoided in the women he became involved with. Physically inexperienced and vulnerable. Family orientated. Warm. Emotional.

Most of all emotional!

In essence she represented everything that Jonas didn't want in his own life.

Yet at the same time, she was everything he *did* want...

He shifted uncomfortably. 'Admittedly, I can't give you romance and flowers, but—'

'I don't remember ever saying I wanted romance and flowers from you!' she cut in indignantly.

Jonas eyed her intently. 'Then what *do* you want, Mac?' he asked bluntly.

'From you?' she asked shortly. 'Nothing.'

'I doubt you would be this...angry, if it was nothing,' Jonas drawled ruefully.

'I'm not in the least angry, Jonas.' Mac sighed. 'At least, not with you.'

'Then who?'

She shook her head. 'You wouldn't understand.'

'Try me,' he invited huskily.

Mac gave a huff of laughter. 'We simply don't look at things the same way, Jonas.'

'Concerning what exactly?'

She almost smiled at the sudden wariness in his expression.

'Concerning everything that matters,' she elaborated. 'I don't need that romance and flowers that you mentioned but I do want my relationships to matter. *I* want to matter!'

'Didn't our lovemaking last night prove that you matter?' he asked.

Mac gave him a pitying glance. 'Last night proved only that you're physically attracted to me.'

'Don't all relationships start that way?'

'All *your* relationships certainly start *and* end that way! As any relationship with me would too,' she added quietly.

'You can't know that—'

'We both know that, Jonas,' she said wearily.

He couldn't let this go. 'You're making assumptions—'

'I'm being realistic,' Mac corrected firmly. 'I really don't want to have an affair with you, Jonas,' she stated honestly.

His mouth twisted. 'Why don't you just come right out and say that you're holding out for the whole package? Love and romance, followed by marriage?'

Mac felt the warmth in her cheek. 'I'm "holding out", as you put it, for exactly what you said I should hold out for last week—the right man to come along.'

'And obviously that isn't me!'

She swallowed down the sick feeling that had risen in her throat. 'Obviously, that isn't you. Don't you see, Jonas, you've allowed your childhood experiences to colour the rest of your life? To damage you rather than anyone else?'

'Are you a psychiatrist too now?' he sneered.

'No, of course not.' She sighed. 'I just think—you'll never be able to function emotionally until you confront the problem you have with your parents.'

'Forgiveness and all that?' he scorned.

'Yes,' she stated.

Jonas stared down at her for long, timeless seconds before breaking that gaze to glance up at the warehouse. 'Have you given any more thought to selling out to Buchanan Construction?'

Mac was thrown for a minute by the sudden change of subject. But only for a minute. 'None at all,' she said definitely.

'Because it isn't going to happen,' Jonas guessed easily.

Mac's chin rose challengingly. 'No.'

Which left Jonas and Buchanan Construction in something of a dilemma. The same dilemma, in fact, that Jonas had been in when he first met Mac over a week ago...

'That's your final word on that subject, too?'

'Absolutely my final word, yes.' She nodded.

Jonas drew in a harsh breath. 'Fine,' he said.

Mac eyed him uncertainly. 'Does that mean you accept my decision?'

He raised dark brows. 'What other choice do I have?'

None as far as Mac was concerned. 'You seemed so—determined to get me out of here a week ago...'

Jonas's smile was as lacking in humour as her own had been a few minutes ago. 'That was before Yvonne started her sick little game.'

'Oh.'

'And before I knew you…' Jonas added softly.

Before Jonas knew her? Or before he 'knew' her in the physical sense?

Did it really matter which, as long as he accepted that she wasn't going to sell the warehouse?

Mac straightened. 'I really do have to go now, Jonas.'

His expression was remote, those eyes a cold, remorseless blue as he nodded. 'Have a pleasant evening.'

Have a pleasant life, he might as well have said, Mac realised achingly.

Because she knew that after today he wanted no part of her or her life. Just as she knew it wasn't specifically her he wanted no part of; it was simply that the very idea of emotional entanglement with anyone was complete anathema to him.

Mac couldn't even imagine what it must be like to live without love in your life. The love of parents. Of family. Of friends. Of that certain special someone that you loved and who loved you.

Although, after today, Mac was going to have to learn to live without the last one herself…

'You too,' she muttered before turning and hurrying up the staircase, her hand shaking slightly as she unlocked the door before going quickly inside and closing it firmly behind her.

Without hesitation.

Without so much as a single backward glance.

Because she dared not look at him again. Knowing that if she did she wouldn't be able to stop herself from launching herself into his arms and agreeing to continue their relationship—that emotionless relationship that was all Jonas could ever give any woman—to its painful conclusion...

Mac lingered only long enough on this floor to drop her keys and helmet on the breakfast bar before hurrying over to switch on the lights to the floor above and ascending the spiral staircase up to her studio.

The canvas she had been working on the last few days still stood on the easel near the glassed wall, the thin cloth Mac had placed over it when she'd brought Jonas up here yesterday evening still in place. After last night she had stayed well away from her studio today, reluctant to see—to be—where the memories of that lovemaking with Jonas were so strong.

Mac crossed the room slowly now to stare at that blank cloth for several seconds before reaching out and removing it.

The background of the painting was there already in shades of blue, but the focus of the painting was only a pencilled sketch at the moment. Strong, abstract lines that nevertheless caught perfectly the wide brow, intensity of light-coloured eyes, high cheekbones either side of an aristocratic slash of a nose, and the mouth sculptured above that square and determined jaw.

Jonas.

Mac rarely painted portraits, and had no idea why she had felt compelled to do this one of him when those hard and handsome features were already etched deep, and for ever, into her soul. As was the love she felt for him.

Painfully.

Irrevocably.

Tears filled Mac's eyes as she continued to stare at that hard and beautiful face on the canvas.

And she wondered what she was going to do with this portrait of Jonas once it was finished.

CHAPTER THIRTEEN

'COME on, Dad, if you don't hurry we're going to be late,' Mac encouraged her father laughingly as the family gathered in the hallway of her parents' bungalow on Christmas Eve to put on their warm coats and hats and scarves in preparation for going out into the cold and snowy evening. 'And you know how Mum hates to be late—' Mac abruptly broke off her teasing as she opened the front door and saw the person standing outside on the doorstep, one of his gloved hands raised as he prepared to ring the doorbell.

Oh, my God, it was Jonas!

Mac felt the colour drain from her face beneath the red woollen hat she wore. Totally stunned as she stared up searchingly into the grimness of Jonas's face. At the scowl between his brows, the guarded blue of his gaze as it met hers, his mouth and jaw set challengingly.

What on earth was he doing here, of all places?

'Jonas.' Mac's gloved fingers tightened painfully on the door as she moistened dry and slightly numbed lips.

He gave a slight inclination of his head before glancing at the people crowding the hallway behind her. 'I realise you weren't expecting me but—am I in time to join you all at church?' he asked huskily.

'I—yes. Of course,' Mac answered haltingly, her thoughts racing as she tried to make sense of Jonas being here at all.

Apart from the man sent by 'the boss' to collect her Jeep and have the windows repaired almost two weeks ago, Mac hadn't seen or heard from Jonas. Nothing. No telephone calls. No sitting on her metal staircase waiting for her to come home. Just an empty…nothing.

If it hadn't been for the continuous ache in her heart, and the vivid memories she had of their lovemaking, Mac might almost have thought that she had imagined him!

Or perhaps she was just imagining he was here now?

Hallucinating might be a better description!

After all, Jonas was sitting on a beach somewhere on a Caribbean island drinking tall drinks adorned with fruit and pretty coloured-paper umbrellas, possibly with a beautiful blonde at his side. Wasn't he?

'Get a move on, darling, or we're— Oh.' Mac's mother came to an abrupt halt beside her to stare up at Jonas with open curiosity.

Not a hallucination, then, Mac acknowledged with a nervous fluttering in her stomach. Jonas really *was* standing on the doorstep of her parents' bungalow at eleven o'clock at night on Christmas Eve!

The look of total disbelief on Mac's expressive face when she had opened the door and found him standing there might have been amusing if Jonas weren't already feeling so totally wrong-footed himself. If he hadn't already been deeply regretting his decision to come to Devon with the stupid idea of surprising her. But as he was feeling both those things he didn't find that look of embarrassed horror on Mac's face in the least reassuring!

'Mrs McGuire.' He extended his hand politely to the woman who, with her short bob of glossy black hair and smoky-grey eyes, bore such a startling resemblance to Mac that she couldn't possibly be anyone else but her mother. 'Jonas Buchanan,' he explained. 'I hope you don't mind my just turning up like this and joining you all for Midnight Mass? I'm—'

'A friend of mine from London,' Mac put in quickly as she moved to stand at Jonas's side before turning to face her family, linking her arm lightly with his as she did so, and looking very festive in a long white overcoat over a red sweater and black jeans. 'I'm so glad you could make it, after all, Jonas,' she assured huskily. 'Mum, Dad, this is Jonas Buchanan. Jonas, my parents, Melly and Brian.'

To give the two elder McGuires their due, they showed no surprise at finding a complete stranger standing on their doorstep at eleven o'clock at night on Christmas Eve, the tall and still-handsome grey-haired Brian moving forward to shake Jonas's hand warmly. 'The more the merrier,' he assured with genuine heartiness. 'I'm afraid we're already late so we'll have to make all the other introductions later,' he added with a rueful smile at the numerous members of Mac's family milling about in the hallway obviously ready to leave for church.

'I can take three other people as well as Mac in my car if that's of any help,' Jonas offered smoothly as Mac's family tumbled outside into the snowy night.

'Perfect,' the beautiful Melly McGuire accepted warmly. 'I won't have to drive the second car now and can have a glass of mulled wine with my mince pie after the service!'

Jonas was preoccupied for the next few minutes helping Mac settle three of her elderly aunts into the back of his car, but conscious all of that time of her puzzled gaze as it rested on him often.

Mac paused out on the icy road. 'Jonas, why aren't you sitting on a beach somewhere on that Caribbean island?' she prompted softly.

Good question.

One that Jonas felt required the two of them being alone when he answered it...

'Never mind,' Mac dismissed as she saw Jonas's hesitation. 'All that matters is you're here.'

He winced slightly. 'Is it?'

'Yes,' Mac answered firmly as she saw that her father had already reversed his car out onto the road and was waiting to leave. 'We had better go,' she said ruefully as she moved to sit in the passenger seat of Jonas's black Mercedes.

Surrounded as they were by so many members of Mac's family, there was absolutely no opportunity for a private conversation between the two of them as they drove the short distance into the village itself, attended the service in the church surrounded by berry-adorned holly and lit by dozens of candles, and then lingered afterwards to chat and enjoy that anticipated mulled wine and those mince pies.

But that didn't mean that Mac wasn't aware of Jonas's presence at her side for that whole time. That she didn't burn with curiosity to know why he was here. And if he intended staying. That her initial uncertainty at seeing him again hadn't begun to turn to hope...

That uncertainty returned with a vengeance once

she and Jonas were finally alone in the sitting-room of her parents' bungalow a little after one o'clock in the morning, the rest of Mac's family having gone to bed. Her mother had already offered the suggestion, 'The small boxroom is empty if Jonas would like to stay for the rest of the Christmas holiday...'

'I did try to warn you,' Mac murmured ruefully as Jonas looked about the sitting-room with its numerous glittering Christmas decorations and enormous and heavily adorned tree with its dozens of presents beneath.

'It's wonderful,' Jonas murmured huskily, his gaze slightly hooded as it came back to rest on Mac as she stood across the room, her hands tightly clasped together in front of her. 'As is your family. I— Mac, I wanted to thank you for my Christmas present,' he said abruptly.

Ah.

Mac smiled a little. 'You didn't have to drive all the way to Devon on Christmas Eve to do that.'

'No.'

Mac shrugged. 'Besides, I had to somehow say thank you for all the help you gave me by having the warehouse painted and the windows on my Jeep fixed. I thought perhaps you might like to hang it in your offices somewhere? In the reception, maybe? A portrait of the head of Buchanan Construction,' she said offhandedly.

'A Mary McGuire portrait of the head of Buchanan Construction,' Jonas corrected softly.

'Well...yes,' she acknowledged awkwardly. 'Just think, if you ever fall on hard times, you'll be able to sell it!' she added jokingly.

Jonas had been surprised when the huge wooden crate was delivered to his office two days ago, stunned when he removed all the packaging and saw the portrait inside. Even so, he hadn't needed to look at the signature in the bottom right hand side of the painting to know it was Mac's work. The style and use of colour were unmistakable.

It was why she had painted it in the first place that Jonas wanted to know...

The last two weeks had been long and...difficult, for Jonas. For numerous reasons. Yvonne Richards. His parents. But most of all, because of Mac.

He hadn't been able to get her out of his mind. Not for a single moment of that time. Her beauty. Her laughter. Her warmth. Her smooth and satiny skin. Her perfume.

This past two weeks Jonas had remembered and re-lived every single moment he had ever spent with her.

As he had always known would happen, memories of Mac had filled his days and haunted his nights!

'I'm not sure I can allow you to give me such a valu-able gift,' he told her gruffly.

Her cheeks flushed. 'I think that's for me to decide, don't you?'

And her temper, Jonas acknowledged ruefully; he hadn't forgotten that fiery temper. How could he, when she had been annoyed or angry with him about one thing or another since the moment they'd first met?

'Yes,' he acknowledged huskily.

Mac's eyes widened. 'Are you actually *agreeing* with me, Jonas?'

He chuckled softly at her obvious incredulity. 'Yes.'

'Well, there's a first!'

Jonas sobered. 'I'm agreeing with you on the under-standing that I be allowed to give you something in return.'

Mac eyed him frowningly. Even dressed casually in a dark blue sweater and faded jeans, Jonas was still the most devastatingly handsome man she had ever met. Several other women in the church earlier tonight had obviously thought the same thing as they had eyed him covetously. Admiring glances that Jonas had seemed completely unaware of as he'd stood attentively at Mac's side, his hand resting lightly beneath her elbow.

She shook her head. 'I already told you, the portrait is a thank you for the way you helped me a couple of weeks ago.' It was also a way for Mac to avoid having Jonas's portrait hanging in her studio as a day-to-day reminder of the man she loved but who would never love her in return...

His mouth tightened. 'Help you wouldn't have needed if—'

'We really don't need to talk about that now, Jonas,' Mac rushed in.

'If you wish.' He gave an abrupt inclination of his head.

'I wish,' Mac confirmed firmly. 'What sort of thing are you giving me in return?' she asked warily.

Jonas thrust his hands into his jeans pockets as he shifted uncomfortably. 'I need to explain a few things first.' He frowned. 'I— You told me when we last met that I needed to confront the problem I have with my parents. That the feelings I have for them were—damaging, to me. That—'

'I seem to have made rather a lot of personal remarks that perhaps I shouldn't!' Mac interrupted uncomfortably. 'I was upset when I said those things, Jonas. You really shouldn't take too much notice of me when I'm upset. I inherited my Irish grandfather's sentimental temperament, I'm afraid.'

Jonas gave a twisted smile. 'The truth is the truth, whenever or however it's said.'

'Not if it's in the heat of the moment—'

'But you were right to say those things to me, Mac,' Jonas insisted softly. 'I *have* allowed my parents' disastrous marriage, my unhappy childhood, to affect the man I am now.' He looked her in the eye. 'I've been to see both my parents during the past two weeks—'

'You have?' Mac gasped.

He nodded. 'I've also met my stepfather and stepmother. I still have nothing in common with any of them,' he continued ruefully. 'But I was with them all long enough to know that both second marriages are happy ones. To learn that my parents no longer feel any animosity towards each other.' He sighed. 'I decided that if they can forgive each other for the past then surely I can forgive them too.'

Mac blinked back the tears that threatened to fall. 'I'm so glad, Jonas. For your sake.'

'Yes,' he said. 'Of course, I consider it completely your fault that this reconciliation has now presented me with another set of problems,' he added dryly.

'My fault?' she echoed. 'How?'

'I now have the diplomatic problem of avoiding offending either of my parents. For example, both sets of parents duly invited me to spend Christmas with them,' he drawled ruefully. 'To have accepted one would have insulted the other.'

Mac repressed a smile. 'So as it's my fault you thought you would come here and bother me instead?'

Jonas looked at her consideringly from beneath hooded lids. 'Am I bothering you, Mac?'

Of course having Jonas here was bothering her! Especially as, avoiding offending either of his parents aside, Mac still had no idea why Jonas had chosen to come here tonight of all nights.

Why he had attended church with her family. What he was still doing here...

She moistened her lips nervously. 'You could always have gone to that beach in the Caribbean,' she reminded him huskily.

'No, I couldn't,' he denied quietly.

'No?'

'No.'

'Why not?' Mac breathed softly, the sudden tension between them so palpable she almost felt as if she could reach out and touch it.

'The only reason that matters,' Jonas murmured.

'Which is?'

He drew in a ragged breath, yet his gaze was clear and unwavering as it met hers. 'The only person I want to spend Christmas with has assured me that under no circumstances would she ever spend Christmas sitting on a beach anywhere!'

Mac couldn't breathe as she stared at him incredulously. *'Me?'* she finally managed to squeak.

Jonas gave a genuine smile. 'You.'

Mac stared at him with wide eyes. 'You want to spend Christmas with *me*?'

'And your family. If you'll allow me to,' he added uncertainly. 'Mac.' He crossed the room in two long strides so that he was now standing only inches away from her. 'I know that I'm— Well, I appreciate that my track record for long-term relationships is—'

'Non-existent,' she put in helpfully as a tidal wave of hope began to build inside her.

Jonas's mouth firmed. 'Non-existent,' he acknowledged. 'But that could be a good thing,' he continued encouragingly as he reached out and grasped both Mac's hands tightly in his. 'It means that I don't have any past relationships, any lingering feelings for another woman, to complicate things.'

That tidal wave of hope grew bigger still as Mac easily saw the lingering uncertainty in Jonas's eyes. 'Complicate what things?' she prompted.

'Ah.' He winced. 'Yes. I need my overcoat from the hallway.' Jonas released her hands. 'Your Christmas present is in the pocket—'

'Family rule, no presents to be unwrapped until Christmas morning!' Mac protested before Jonas could leave the sitting-room.

He turned in the doorway. 'It already *is* Christmas morning, Mac,' he pointed out dryly. 'Besides, this present isn't gift-wrapped,' he added confidently.

Mac had no idea what was going on. Just now Jonas had seemed on the point of—well, on the point of something. And now he was totally preoccupied with giving her a Christmas present instead.

When the only Christmas present Mac wanted was Jonas himself!

Jonas returned from the hallway to find Mac still standing where he had left her. His heart pounded loudly in his chest as he walked over to join her, two folded sheets of paper in his hand. 'I'd like your input on this before I submit it for planning approval.' His expression was strained as he handed her the top sheet of paper.

Mac gave him an uncertain glance before she slowly unfolded the sheet of paper, a frown between her eyes as she looked up at him. 'I— It appears to be a building plan of the new apartment complex, one that rather tastefully incorporates my warehouse into the grounds...'

A nerve pulsed in the tenseness of Jonas's jaw. 'It *is*

a building plan of the new apartment complex that—hopefully—tastefully incorporates your warehouse,' he confirmed huskily.

She refolded it carefully. 'And the other one?' She looked at the second sheet of design paper in Jonas's hand.

Jonas's fingers tightened perceptibly. 'These are some alterations to the original plan that don't include your warehouse in the grounds.'

Mac looked at him accusingly as she thrust the original sheet back into his hands. 'And *this* is the present you drove all this way to give me?' she exclaimed. 'You're unbelievable, do you know that, Jonas?' She looked thoroughly disgusted. 'You've come all this way just to have yet another attempt at trying to talk me into selling my home!' She moved away restlessly. 'The answer is no, Jonas. N. O. Is that clear enough for you?' Angry tears glistened in those smoky-grey eyes as she glared at him.

Well that went well, Jonas—*not*! he told himself, wincing. Self-confident to the point of arrogance usually, he had known before he came here tonight that he was somehow going to bungle this. Because it was more important than anything else had ever been in his life before. Because it mattered to him more than anything else ever had in his life before!

'I haven't asked the question yet...' he murmured softly.

'You don't need to,' Mac fired back. 'Just leave, Jonas. Go away and never come back. I never want to see—'

'Mac, will you marry me?'

'—or speak to you *ever*—' Mac abruptly broke off her tirade to stare across at him incredulously. 'What did you just say?'

Jonas swallowed hard. 'I asked if you would do me the honour of marrying me,' he repeated gruffly as he moved hesitantly towards her, the intensity of his gaze searching the paleness of Mac's face as he stood in front of her.

Exactly what she had thought he'd said!

She looked closely at his face, finally seeing the anxiety in those blue eyes, in his tensely clenched jaw and cheeks. 'Why?' she breathed.

Jonas gave a huff of laughter. 'Most women would have said, "No, thank you, Jonas," or, "Oh, Jonas this is so sudden." You, being you, ask me *why*!' He gave a rueful shake of his head.

Mac gave him an irritated glance. 'Well, it *is* rather sudden.'

'Not to me.' Jonas sighed. 'The two weeks since we were last together have been—' He shook his head. 'Hell, is the only fitting description I can think of,' he decided heavily.

'Why?'

'Again with the why!' He briefly raised his gaze to the ceiling. 'Mac, I didn't *want* to fall in love with you. It's the last thing I ever wanted! But you—' He sighed. 'You are the most infuriating, provoking, stubborn, irritating—'

'Do you think we could go back to the "I didn't want to fall in love with you" bit...?' Mac interrupted, her heart beating so loudly, so erratically, she was sure Jonas must be able to hear it too.

'—fascinating, warm, arousing, wonderful woman I have ever met!' Jonas finished. 'How could I not fall in love with you?' He shook his head as he once again reached out to grasp both Mac's hands in his.

Mac felt hot and cold all at the same time. 'You really love me?' she breathed dazedly.

'It's worse than that, I'm afraid,' Jonas muttered. 'Mac, this past two weeks I've come to realise that I want it *all* with you. Love. Marriage. Children. I want to be your last lover as well as your first. I want to wake up and find you beside me for the rest of my life. Most of all I want to be the man you deserve. The man you can love. Will you at least give me the chance to show you that I can be that man?' He looked down at her anxiously.

Jonas loved her! Wanted to marry her! Have children with her!

Mac released one of her hands from his to reach up tentatively and cup one hard and chiselled cheek. 'Are you sure about this, Jonas? Absolutely sure? Love, marriage, children—those things mean for ever to me, you know...'

His fingers tightened painfully about hers. 'I wouldn't settle for anything less!' he assured her fiercely. 'Mac, you totally misunderstood my motives for those two new sets of plans. The first one leaves the warehouse standing, yes, but the second one shows a completely different layout to the penthouse in the apartment complex.'

'Show me,' she encouraged huskily.

Jonas unfolded and smoothed out the second set of plans. 'You see here?' He pointed to the diagram. 'That wall is now completely glass, as is the ceiling in that room. It's a replica of your studio, Mac,' he explained gruffly. 'I went to see my parents because I love you. Because you were right about my needing to confront that situation, to deal with those ghosts from the past, before I could move on with my own life. You are my life, Mac. I'm asking you to give me the chance to show you that, to prove to you how much I love you. To show you how I will always love you, and only you. Exactly as you are,' he added emphatically.

'No dressing up and being a trophy on your arm, then?' she teased a little tearfully.

Jonas really did love her!

'As far as I'm concerned you can live in those damn-awful dungarees and never set foot outside the apartment again as long as I can be there with you. Mac, just give me the chance to show you how much I love you, to persuade you into falling in love with me, and I promise you won't ever have reason to regret it!' he vowed.

'Oh, Jonas,' she groaned.

He gave a pained wince. 'Is that a "no, thank you, Jonas," or a "Let me think about this, Jonas."?'

'It's an "I already love you, Jonas,"' Mac assured him emotionally as she moved into his arms.

'You *love* me?' There was a look of stunned disbelief on his face.

'So much that I really don't care where I live any more, either, as long as it's with you! Jonas, I love you so much that these past two weeks have been hell for me too. I love you, Jonas!' she repeated joyfully.

His arms moved about her like steel bands. 'Enough to marry me?'

'Enough to spend for ever, eternity, with you!' she assured him happily.

Jonas looked down at her searchingly for long, time-less minutes, his eyes blazing with his love for her as he saw that emotion reflected back at him. He buried his face in the perfume of her silky hair as he groaned. 'I can't believe that I let you walk away from me two weeks ago. That I almost lost you!'

'Just kiss me, Jonas,' Mac encouraged breathlessly.

'I intend to kiss you and love you for the rest of our lives,' he promised as his mouth finally claimed hers.

The rest of their lives sounded just perfect to Mac...

MILLS & BOON®
HAVE JOINED FORCES
WITH THE LEANDER TRUST
AND LEANDER CLUB TO HELP
TO DEVELOP TOMORROW'S
CHAMPIONS

We have produced a stunning calendar for 2011 featuring a host of Olympic and World Champions (as they've never been seen before!). Leander Club is recognised the world over for its extraordinary rowing achievements and is committed to developing its squad of athletes to help underpin future British success at World and Olympic level.

'All my rowing development has come through the support and back-up from Leander. The Club has taken me from a club rower to an Olympic Silver Medallist. Leander has been the driving force behind my progress'

RIC EGINGTON – Captain, Leander Club Olympic Silver, Beijing, 2009 World Champion.

ALL PROCEEDS TO THE LEANDER TRUST

NAÏVE BRIDE, DEFIANT WIFE

by Lynne Graham

Alejandro Vasquez has never forgotten—nor forgiven—his runaway wife. When he discovers Jemima's whereabouts, and that he has a son, he'll settle the score…

STRANDED, SEDUCED…PREGNANT

by Kim Lawrence

The brooding Italian Severo Constanza comes to Neve Macleod's rescue knowing nothing of her scandalous past— just that he will delight in taking her as his own!

INNOCENT VIRGIN, WILD SURRENDER

by Anne Mather

On a quest to find her mother, Rachel Claiborne is distracted by the irresistible Matt Brody, who is clearly keeping secrets. Rachel must *not* give in to temptation…

CAPTURED AND CROWNED

by Janette Kenny

When Kristo Stanrakis takes his brother's fiancée for his queen, he realises Demetria is the unforgettable stranger with whom, years ago, he nearly made love. Now the king is determined to finish what he started!

On sale from 19th November 2010
Don't miss out!

Available at WHSmith, Tesco, ASDA, Eason and all good bookshops

www.millsandboon.co.uk

NICOLO: THE POWERFUL SICILIAN
by Sandra Marton

She knew the Orsini name meant danger, but Alessia Antoninni was unprepared for Nicolo Orsini's lethal good looks. Soon, dangerously close to giving in to his demands, her heart *and* her business are at risk...

SHOCK: ONE-NIGHT HEIR
by Melanie Milburne

Giorgio Sabbatini must maintain the family line. Unable to give him an heir, wife Maya knows she has to walk away. But she can't resist one last night of passion...

HER LAST NIGHT OF INNOCENCE
by India Grey

After a near-fatal crash, racing driver Cristiano Maresca lost his memory. Now Kate Edwards must tell Italy's most notorious playboy he has a love-child!

BUTTONED-UP SECRETARY, BRITISH BOSS
by Susanne James

Alexander McDonald finds his new secretary Sabrina Gold tantalising. Having vowed never to mix business and pleasure, he's suddenly tempted to break his own rules...

On sale from 3rd December 2010
Don't miss out!

Available at WHSmith, Tesco, ASDA, Eason and all good bookshops

www.millsandboon.co.uk

THE *Balfour* LEGACY

EIGHT SISTERS, EIGHT SCANDALS

VOLUME 5 – OCTOBER 2010
Zoe's Lesson
by Kate Hewitt

VOLUME 6 – NOVEMBER 2010
Annie's Secret
by Carole Mortimer

VOLUME 7 – DECEMBER 2010
Bella's Disgrace
by Sarah Morgan

VOLUME 8 – JANUARY 2011
Olivia's Awakening
by Margaret Way

8 VOLUMES IN ALL TO COLLECT!

2 FREE BOOKS
AND A SURPRISE GIFT

We would like to take this opportunity to thank you for reading this Mills & Boon® book by offering you the chance to take TWO more specially selected books from the Modern™ series absolutely FREE! We're also making this offer to introduce you to the benefits of the Mills & Boon® Book Club™—

- **FREE home delivery**
- **FREE gifts and competitions**
- **FREE monthly Newsletter**
- **Exclusive Mills & Boon Book Club offers**
- **Books available before they're in the shops**

Accepting these FREE books and gift places you under no obligation to buy, you may cancel at any time, even after receiving your free books. Simply complete your details below and return the entire page to the address below. You don't even need a stamp!

YES Please send me 2 free Modern books and a surprise gift. I understand that unless you hear from me, I will receive 4 superb new books every month for just £3.30 each, postage and packing free. I am under no obligation to purchase any books and may cancel my subscription at any time. The free books and gift will be mine to keep in any case.

Ms/Mrs/Miss/Mr _____ Initials _____

Surname _____

Address _____

_____ Postcode _____

E-mail _____

Send this whole page to: Mills & Boon Book Club, Free Book Offer, FREEPOST NAT 10298, Richmond, TW9 1BR